Be
Light
Like
a
Bird

Be Light Like a Bird is published by Capstone Young Readers
A Capstone Imprint
1710 Roe Crest Drive
North Mankato, Minnesota 56003
www.mycapstone.com

Text © 2016 by Monika Schröder

Library of Congress Cataloging-in-Publication Data

Names: Schröder, Monika, 1965- author.
Title: Be light like a bird / by Monika Schröder.
Description: North Mankato, Minnesota : Stone Arch Books, a Capstone imprint, [2016] | Summary: When her father is killed in an accident, twelve-year-old Wren is grief stricken, but what upsets her even more is that her mother seems to be filled with anger, rather than sadness--as they move from place to place Wren is forced to cope with her mother's strange behavior, her own grief, and all the problems that come with being the new girl in Michigan's Upper Peninsula, where they finally end up.
Identifiers: LCCN 2015046433| ISBN: 9781623707491 (paper over board) |
   ISBN 9781496533012 (library hardcover) | ISBN 9781496533029 (ebook pdf)
Subjects: LCSH: Mothers and daughters--Juvenile fiction. | Grief--Juvenile
   fiction. | Bereavement--Juvenile fiction. | Moving, Household--
   Juvenile fiction. | Adjustment (Psychology)--Juvenile fiction. | Bird
   watching--Juvenile fiction. | Upper Peninsula (Mich.)--Juvenile fiction. |
   CYAC: Mothers and daughters--Fiction. | Grief--Fiction. | Moving,
   Household--Fiction. | Conduct of life--Fiction. | Bird watching--Fiction. |
   Upper Peninsula (Mich.)--Fiction.
Classification: LCC PZ7.S37955 Be 2016 | DDC [Fic]--dc23
LC record available at http://lccn.loc.gov/2015046433

Editor: Alison Deering
Book Designer: Kay Fraser
Photo Credits: Vector images by Shutterstock

Lyrics excerpted from *Stranger Music* by Leonard Cohen. Copyright © 1993 Leonard Cohen. Reprinted by permission of McClelland & Stewart, a division of Penguin Random House Canada Limited.

Textual excerpt from Walt Disney Television Animation's *Pooh's Grand Adventure: The Search for Christopher Robin*. Reprinted by permission of Disney Enterprises, Inc.

The title of this book comes from the quote: "One should be light like a bird, and not like a feather." / "Il faut être léger comme l'oiseau, et non comme la plume" — Paul Valéry, Choses Tues (1930)

Printed in China.
010208R

Be Light Like a Bird

BY MONIKA SCHRÖDER

Capstone Young Readers
a capstone imprint

This one was still intact. No innards splashed out or bloody tire tracks on the asphalt. Lying on its side, with its legs stiff and the bushy tail forming a perfect curve, the squirrel could have been some kid's cute stuffed animal, except for the small puddle of blood oozing from its open mouth.

I got off my bike, pulled on my rubber gloves, and took the trowel from my backpack. It was quiet on 8 Mile Road. No one would see me. The two horses, grazing in the pasture behind me, paid no attention to what I was doing. The soil by the side of the road was moist, easy to dig. I nudged the squirrel with my index finger onto the trowel. When its head rolled back, more blood trickled onto the pavement. My stomach cramped. I hated the blood.

There was no smell of death on this one yet so I didn't need to hold my breath as I placed the squirrel in the ground and covered it with dirt. Then I inhaled, waiting for that moment when having done this made me feel better.

But that moment didn't come.

I jumped back onto my bike and rode on as fast as I could, not letting up until my lungs burned. I'd never counted how many animals I'd buried since Dad died. I didn't make a list or anything. I wasn't that crazy.

1

It wasn't the crash that killed my dad when his plane went down over the Atlantic. He died from hypoxia, a state of oxygen deficiency that impairs brain function. And it wasn't *his* airplane. We aren't the kind of people who own airplanes. Ma used to work in an old folks' home, and Dad drove a FedEx truck but dreamed of getting a pilot's license. He was with his flight instructor, who actually flew the plane.

They took off from Marietta on a clear, crisp Sunday in February. After takeoff, something must have gone wrong. They didn't notice the drop in air pressure in the Learjet's cabin. Or maybe they did but couldn't do anything about it because they didn't have any extra oxygen onboard. The plane kept climbing right through its assigned altitude while flying east toward the Atlantic coast.

Once you rise above twelve thousand feet in a depressurized cabin, it takes only twelve minutes to lose consciousness. I never knew that.

On the evening news an Air Force pilot said that the jet was "porpoising" while it fluctuated between fifteen thousand and forty thousand feet. As in the way dolphins move through the water. I wished they hadn't used that word.

The search-and-rescue team told us that Dad and the instructor had most likely blacked out long before the plane ran out of fuel and dropped thirty thousand feet. They said Dad and the pilot didn't feel the impact. I hoped they were right.

* * *

After the search-and-rescue people called, there was an explosion in my brain, and a cloud appeared, spreading out over everything. The cloud pressed down on me like overstuffed down bedding, the kind you want to push away so you can breathe. Except there was nothing I could do to lift it. The cloud made all my thoughts seem as though they came through a fun-house mirror, like the one Dad and I had stood in front of at the county fair last year, laughing. Everything was distorted, drawn into longer, thinner shapes; or shorter, wider ones; or ones with missing pieces. But now, the effect was disturbing rather than funny. It made it hard to think.

It was because of the cloud that I didn't notice at first how much Ma had changed. I didn't remember her often being angry before. She had always been the more practical of my parents. But given her cooking skills, it actually wasn't that practical of her to turn down the casseroles that her coworkers from the nursing home tried to drop off at our house in the week following Dad's death.

"We really won't need those," she'd say, standing at the door with a fake smile whenever someone came by.

"Couldn't we take at least one?" I asked when the two of us were alone. "We could have thrown it out if we didn't like it." Not that I was particularly hungry. But food would have been a welcome distraction from the cloud.

"I don't want these people's food," Ma said, a dangerous edge in her voice. "They just want to make themselves feel better."

If Dad were still here, he would have told us that there was nothing wrong with helping others. "So one good deed makes two people feel better," he would have said. "What's not to like?"

Perhaps Ma would have shaken her head at him, smiling. She actually used to shake her head often at him, but in a loving way. Like when she called him a dreamer, and Dad said, "Oh no, my dear. I am a seeker of possibilities."

It hurt to think that it would never be like that again. Never.

2

The only person who came to mourn with us was Ma's younger brother, Huey. And he only found out because he happened to call that week.

"You can't stay long!" was pretty much the first thing Ma said to him when he arrived. Even though she knew he had to stay at least one night since he lived in Texas, an eight-hour drive away.

"They didn't find him?" Uncle Huey asked.

"No," Ma said with that new bitterness in her voice. "They searched three days, but the plane crashed over deep water. They'll probably never find a thing." She let out a sarcastic laugh.

Uncle Huey took out a leather pouch and rolled himself a cigarette.

"You can't smoke in here," Ma said sharply.

"I know. I know," he said, rolling his eyes. "Chillax, sis. You've gotta have at least, like, a memorial service or something." He looked at me. "Wren needs, you know, some kind of closure."

"There won't be a funeral," Ma said. "Or anything else for that matter."

"You can't just move on, sis."

"We're okay," Ma said. She shot him a look that made him lower his head and study his woolen socks.

But I wasn't okay, and Ma wasn't either. Dad's death had changed both of us. The cloud was pressing down on me, while Ma had turned angry and distant.

Later we ordered pizza and watched a cheesy movie on the Disney channel. Uncle Huey didn't try to make any more conversation, but stepped out into the garden several times to smoke. When he came back and didn't wipe his feet on the doormat, Ma yelled at him. She made him put his beer on a coaster too. Uncle Huey just sighed, and soon Ma went upstairs to her room, slamming the door behind her. A few minutes later we could hear her pacing back and forth above us.

It felt good to just sit there with Uncle Huey, even without talking. Three days had passed since the phone call, and by that point I had cried more than I thought possible.

When I went up to bed, I found three garbage bags with Dad's clothes in the hallway. From my bedroom window I saw Ma outside, throwing a bunch of papers onto the grill. Then she lit them on fire.

* * *

The following week there was a problem with the mortgage. Apparently Dad had spent all of our savings trying to get a pilot's license, and he hadn't paid the bank for the past few months. When Ma learned that we would be evicted before the end of the month, she cried.

At first, I was actually glad to see her show some emotion, because she hadn't cried at all since it happened. But when she started throwing Dad's model airplanes against the wall, I realized she wasn't crying because she was sad — it was because she was so mad.

Then she told me to put everything I wanted to keep into a suitcase.

How do you decide what to keep when your Dad has died and your mother has turned into a raging woman you hardly recognize? If it were up to me, I would have kept everything the way it was before. But that was obviously not an option.

Ma continued to be angry at Dad's stuff — even his furniture. She called some guy who came and emptied Dad's study. Just before he packed it all up, I managed to save Dad's bird-watching binoculars. His were better than mine. Then I sat in my room and looked around, trying to decide what to pack, but the cloud was making me numb. None of the stuff really mattered anymore.

Next to my bed was my bird book. But how could I ever watch birds again? That had always been Dad's and my thing. I loved those weekend mornings when he wouldn't go to flight school, and we'd go out to look for birds instead.

I let my hand glide over the soft leather cover of the birding journal Dad had given me last year for my twelfth birthday. On the first page, in the little box with two lines, I had asked Dad to write my name in his nice cursive: *Wren Kaiser*, with a little loop on the *W* and a tiny straight line above the *i*. He had written it with the fountain pen Ma and I had given him for **his** birthday. We'd made a special trip to a fancy store in Atlanta where they only sold fountain pens, some of them for more than a thousand dollars. The one we'd picked was shiny black with a golden tip and a marbled cap, and only cost a hundred dollars. That was still a lot of money for us, but Dad had loved that pen and had carried it with him all the time.

I suddenly remembered to look for it, but by then the guy had already taken all of Dad's stuff. I ran downstairs to tell Ma that the fountain pen was gone. "We should have kept that at least," I said.

"It's better this way," Ma said. When I tried to protest she threw me her angry look and said, "It's **gone!**"

I walked back to my room, tears in my eyes. I didn't understand. Why would she yell at me now?

Before he'd left, Uncle Huey had told me her anger was only a phase and that Ma would act normal again soon. "She's just shutting down for a while," he'd said. "Just leave her be, and she'll snap out of it."

I wished I had asked Uncle Huey how long it would be until she snapped out of it. I was ready for her to talk to me about Dad *now*. I wanted her to hug me. I wanted us to cry together. I didn't want to be alone with all this pain.

Back in my room, I put the bird book and journal in my suitcase and filled the rest with clothes. Then I stuffed my shoes into a plastic bag.

The next morning we bolted north on I-75 in Dad's old car, a Volvo station wagon. It was the only thing of his Ma had kept.

"A fresh start," she said.

Even that sounded angry.

3

Our first stop was Chattanooga, Tennessee. For years Ma had been taking care of elderly people back in Georgia, and she quickly found work in a nursing home. We moved into a furnished apartment, and I joined sixth grade.

Being the new girl at school was hard. Not that I used to have a lot of friends back home. Fitting in at school had been hard for me even before Dad died. I had never hung out with the popular crowd, and I didn't have a best friend. It was more that I tried hanging out with different girls, rather than just one group, but it never came easy to me. Bird-watching was just not the kind of hobby that made you popular in sixth grade.

"Please, don't mention Dad," I told Ma when she registered me at the new school in Chattanooga. "I don't want them to know yet. If they do they will make a big deal out of it."

"No problem," Ma said. I knew she would understand. She didn't want to talk about Dad either.

On my first day of school, Ma dropped me off. We'd brought my bike from Georgia, but it was raining too heavily for me to ride it. I waited for her to say something, like, "Good luck," or "Hope you have a good first day," but she seemed absentminded and eager to get away.

Feeling lost, I watched her drive off. The cloud made me raw, like I had lost an outer layer of skin, and everything reminded me of Dad. As I was walking toward the entrance, I saw another girl being dropped off at school by her father, and I had to run to the bathroom to cry.

On the second day, Mrs. McKee, my new homeroom teacher, made me stay after school. "I saw you stayed all by yourself during recess," she said. "Should we assign a buddy to you?"

"No," I said. "I don't want a buddy. I'm fine. I'm just shy."

"You need to make a friend," she said. "It can be hard to be new at a school."

You need to make a friend. I almost laughed at her. How do you make a friend if you don't know when you might have to run to the bathroom to cry? Being new wasn't even my biggest problem. I couldn't tell anyone about Dad. I didn't want to become like Cynthia, a girl at my old school. She had been super popular and a really good writer, but then her mother had died suddenly. After our teacher had told the class about her mother's death, no one wanted Cynthia to be his or her peer-editor in language arts. Robyn, her best friend, stayed with her, but I'd watched them on the playground, and they hardly ever talked.

That's why I didn't want anyone in the new school to know about Dad. You mention that someone close to you died, and everyone thinks you're contaminated with death. It makes people feel uncomfortable. They don't know what to say. They might pretend to care, but the truth is, your sadness sticks to you like skunk-stink. You might as well have leprosy.

On my third day at the new school I noticed that my science teacher had hair on the backs of his hands, and the only thing I could do for the rest of the morning was try to remember what Dad's hands had looked like. When I came home I asked Ma.

"I don't know," she said shortly.

"Doesn't it bother you that you can't remember?" I asked.

"No," was all she said.

"I don't believe you," I said.

"Well, that's your choice," Ma answered in a tone that made it clear she was done with the topic.

It was quiet then, with just the refrigerator hum filling the silence between us. Some people say there's an elephant in the room when there's something between two people they don't want to talk about. Our elephant was a 35-year-old man, sitting unconscious in the cockpit of a small jet, about to crash into the Atlantic Ocean.

4

After we had been in Tennessee for about a week, Ma took on a second job as a waitress in the evenings. I hardly ever saw her anymore after that.

"Why are you working at night now too?" I asked.

"Because we need the money," Ma said.

But I knew the truth — she was busy getting over Dad's death without ever feeling sad, and didn't want to stay home with me and my grief.

After only a few days at her new job, Ma came home one evening whistling.

"Are you okay?" I asked.

"More than okay," she said. "I met someone, and he's taking me out for dinner."

I didn't understand how that would make her happy. But then after she'd left the house wearing a short skirt and too much makeup, I started to get this cold feeling in my stomach.

I stayed up waiting for Ma to come back. I didn't like the furnished apartment she was renting for us. An earlier renter must have smoked, and the smell still clung to the curtains. But there was a TV with cable, and I passed the time flipping through the channels.

It was almost midnight when I heard a car park in front of the apartment complex. From behind the curtain, I watched Ma climb out of the passenger seat of an unfamiliar car. The man driving got out too and walked her to the entrance. He was older than Dad and wore a tie. Dad had never worn ties. He hadn't even owned any except for the one with little pink airplanes on it that I had given him last Christmas as a joke.

The man with the tie walked Ma to the door, and I watched them stand there for a while, talking in low voices. Then the most unbelievable thing happened — they kissed!

I had to calm my breathing, and when Ma came back into the apartment I confronted her. "How can you even do that?"

"Do what?" Ma asked.

"Kiss another man."

"He's very nice," she said, but I could tell she felt awkward at having been caught.

"So you're dating another man already? After such a short amount of time?" I asked. "It hasn't even been a month since Dad died."

Ma shook her head. "You don't understand."

"Exactly. I don't understand," I said quietly. "You're betraying Dad. It would hurt him to know you didn't even take time to be sad about him being gone first."

"Betray your dad? That's almost funny," Ma said with that sarcastic laughter I had heard the first time the day she burned his papers.

"It's not funny, it's . . ." I couldn't find the right words. Finally I swallowed and asked, "Are you in love with this new man?"

"Wren, you don't know anything about love," she said without looking at me.

"I do, too," I insisted. "I know I loved Dad." I wanted to add that I also knew I loved Ma — or at least that I wanted to love her, but she was making it hard.

But Ma wouldn't let me finish. "Let's not talk about this anymore. I'm sorry this upset you. That's the way things are. We have to move on — both of us."

* * *

The next morning I buried my first roadkill. It was a cold, clear day, and I was biking back from the grocery store. I had seen roadkill before and always turned away. But this time it was different. When I saw the kitten by the side of the road, already bloated, its hind legs and tail a bloody mess, it felt like when you read one of those word problems in math over and over without any clue how to solve it, and then, suddenly, you know exactly what to do.

I got off my bike, stuffed the contents of one of my shopping bags into the other, and picked up the kitten with the empty bag. Then I pedaled home, the bag with the dead cat dangling from my handlebars. Ma was at work, so I knew I wouldn't have to explain myself. I dropped the groceries on the counter, took a large serving spoon from the kitchen drawer, and went back outside. I chose a spot under the manicured hedge in the far corner of the parking lot to dig a hole.

Once the kitten was buried, I took a deep breath. For a moment the cloud disappeared, and I didn't feel so lonely anymore. It gave me hope. Maybe my thinking would get clear again if I just kept doing what I felt I had to do. But I could already feel the cloud's shadow creeping closer. To escape for a bit longer, I ran as fast as I could all the way up the stairs to the eighth floor.

By the time I was back in the apartment my heart was pounding. Every breath felt like a stab with a sharp blade. But as I washed my hands, watching the dirty water swirl into the drain, a tiny piece of my sadness disappeared.

5

Two days later I did it again. I buried a robin I found by the side of the road, already picked over by crows. Now that I had started paying attention, I suddenly saw roadkill much more frequently than I used to. To be prepared for their burials, I started carrying gloves and a trowel in my backpack at all times.

Three days later Ma wanted to leave Chattanooga.

"It'll be a new start," she said.

"*Another* new start?" I asked. "We've been here for less than three weeks."

But Ma just ignored me and started to pack up the few things we had brought with us from Georgia.

"Why are we moving all the time now?" I asked as I began to throw my clothes into my backpack. "When we lived in Marietta you never even wanted to go on a weekend trip."

"That's because we didn't have the money," Ma said. "And this is not a vacation. We have to find another place to live."

I didn't want to ask about her boyfriend — or whatever you call a man who dates your mother only three weeks after she becomes a widow — but I figured he was probably one of the reasons she didn't want to stay in Chattanooga. I actually didn't mind leaving too much. I hadn't gotten used to the new school yet, and I didn't like the apartment. Plus, it was easier to think about Dad in the car than at school, where the teacher would interrupt me when she thought I wasn't paying attention.

Back in the Volvo, I searched the glove compartment where Dad used to keep his mints.

"I threw them out," Ma said.

As we turned onto I-75, Ma switched on the radio while I replayed our last morning together with Dad. I used to love our Sunday mornings, but that one had been different. Dad had made pancakes, and Ma had complained about the mess he'd left in the kitchen. After I'd helped him clean up, they'd gotten in a fight over a splash of batter on the microwave door. She wasn't usually that picky, and I wondered if she felt bad about that now.

"Do you ever think about the last time you saw him?" I asked, turning the volume down on a Beatles song. "Dad, I mean."

"No," Ma said. "And you shouldn't either. It only hurts you more."

"You had a fight that morning before he left for flight school," I said. "You got mad at him about pancake batter."

I could see by the way Ma's knuckles turned white that she was gripping the steering wheel tighter. "Did you hear what I just said? I don't want to think about it."

"Why are you so angry?" I pressed. "You can't be angry at him for dying. It wasn't his fault."

"I am not angry," Ma said. She turned the volume back up, leaving me under the cloud, thinking about Dad. I was lonely, even with her sitting right next to me.

* * *

At a rest stop in Wapakoneta, Ohio, Ma ripped out an ad in the paper for a job in a nursing home. They hired her that afternoon, and a few hours later, we moved into Fountain Hills, Apartment 4B. The next day I was the new girl at a new school once more.

Father — deceased, Ma wrote on the school application form this time. Once they found out it was a "recent loss," they made me see Mrs. Gonzales, the school counselor. I didn't want to talk about how I felt with someone who didn't even know me. She wouldn't understand the cloud, and I didn't think Mrs. Gonzales really cared for me anyway. Her phone *pinged* constantly, and I could tell she would rather be checking her messages than be with me. But she told me about stages of grief, and when she said one of them was anger I listened up.

"Why would someone get angry at a dead person?" I asked.

"Well," she said, peeking at her phone one more time, "after the grieving person realizes that they cannot deny what happened, they often become angry that this happened to them."

"But you can't get mad at a person for dying in an accident. It makes no sense," I said. "It's not his fault that he died."

"Things don't always make sense when it comes to grieving," Mrs. Gonzales said.

"How long does a person stay in the anger stage?" I asked.

"That depends," she replied.

"On what?"

"On the person. You might be angry for a week, while your mother might be angry for much longer."

During my next class, social studies, I thought about what Mrs. Gonzales had said, but I still couldn't make any sense of it. According to her, the first stage of grief was denial — pretending it hadn't happened. Neither Ma nor I had experienced that. I knew for a fact that Ma wasn't pretending Dad hadn't died. She'd very clearly known the accident had happened when she'd thrown away all his stuff, burned the papers, and made us leave our home.

I wondered if the stages were just something people who'd never lost someone had invented.

I tried to focus on the lesson my class was working on — a unit about the difference between needs and wants — but the lists the teacher made didn't really include the things I needed or wanted. I *wanted* to talk with Ma about what had happened, but she avoided the subject. I *needed* the cloud to lift so I could think clearly and make her talk to me. But for now my head was full of memories of Dad that swirled around like dead leaves blown in the wind.

At least I didn't need to work hard to keep up in school. I'd always been a fairly good student — not the best in class, but with grades that caused no concern among my teachers or parents. Dad had always teased me when I showed him an *A*. He would tickle me gently and say, "Look at you, Little Lady Genius. You must have gotten that from your mother." Ma would laugh at him and tell me that she was proud of me. Sometimes she'd add that I shouldn't pay any attention to a slacker like Dad, but she'd say it with a smile so we knew she was kidding.

But then I remembered a few weeks before Dad had died, when I'd gotten an *A+* on my science test. Dad had held up my test and said, "Karen, look at this. We might have a future Nobel Prize winner on our hands."

Ma had lost her sense of humor and her response had been harsh. "I really don't know what your problem is, Derek," she'd shot back. "It wouldn't be too bad if *someone* in this family had a successful career."

They'd both been quiet for a moment before Dad had left the room. I'd felt bad, because I could see that he was hurt by her comment. I wasn't sure why Ma had said it. Maybe she'd been disappointed that he hadn't gotten the promotion he'd talked about. When I'd mentioned it to Dad at our next bird-watching outing he'd just said, "Don't worry about it. Your mother and I just have to duke out some issues. That's all. Happens to the best of people."

Now I wondered if they'd ever *duked it out*. But I knew better than to ask. Ma wouldn't want to talk about *that* either.

6

We had only been in Ohio for a week when I saw Ma with a new Mr. Someone. This man was also older than Dad, and he picked her up in a black BMW. As they drove off, I noticed an Audubon Society sticker on his rear window. That piqued my interest for a moment as I thought he might be a bird-watcher, but then I realized that didn't matter. I wouldn't talk to him anyway.

But then the next day I met him. My after-school activity got canceled, and I came home earlier than usual. Ma was home, and Mr. Someone was just about to leave. From close up he looked really old, with gray hair and wrinkly skin on his neck.

"This is George," Ma said. I was so surprised to see him that I couldn't say anything.

"Hi, kiddo," George said. On his way to the door he gave me this look of sympathy, like he wanted to say, *I know what you are going through. It's really hard. I'm sorry.*

The look and what I thought it meant made the cloud so heavy it almost suffocated me. I didn't want this man feeling sorry for me. I didn't want this man in our apartment. Ma must have told him about Dad. Maybe she'd told him how she felt. How could she talk to a stranger about him but not me?

After the man was gone, I looked at Ma. For a few seconds I imagined her face was melting — that she would now cry with me and we would share memories of Dad and things would get better and Mr. Someone would never come back. I loved her so much in that moment.

I stepped toward Ma, but the softness disappeared, and she checked her watch. "I'd better hurry, or I'll be late for work. There's lasagna in the microwave for you."

After she left, I thought again about what Mrs. Gonzales had told me about the stages of grief and how time was supposed to heal all wounds. Time hadn't healed anything for me. If there were any stages of grief, I was stuck in the one that hurts and hurts and puts you in a sticky cloud that muddles your brain. For Ma, time seemed to have healed all wounds already. She only seemed to experience two stages of grief — falling in and out of love as quickly as she could.

* * *

Three days later, I heard Ma yelling at Mr. Audubon outside. Soon after, she stormed into the house, locked herself in the bathroom, and blew her nose.

I knew what was coming.

When they teach cause-and-effect relationships in social studies class, this would be a perfect example. Soon after Ma's first date, there's some kind of drama, followed by a breakup — cause — and we move — effect.

The next day we headed back out onto I-75.

7

"Where are we going now?" I asked, looking at the map. We had been driving for five hours and had just passed Grayling, Michigan.

"I don't know," Ma said. "I guess we'll just keep going."

"If we keep driving north we'll end up in Canada," I said.

"We won't go to Canada," she said.

By the time we crossed the Mackinaw Bridge it was getting dark. I checked the map again. Soon we'd reach the end of I-75, all the way up in Michigan's Upper Peninsula, at the city of Sault Ste. Marie. From there it was only a short drive across a bridge to get to Canada. But just a few miles west of Sault Ste. Marie I noticed a town called Pyramid.

"There's a place called Pyramid," I said. "We could stop there."

To my surprise, Ma nodded. "All right."

* * *

You'd think someplace named Pyramid would at least have a hill that looked remotely like the ancient monuments in Egypt. But this close to Lake Superior, the landscape was just flat. A marker on the way into town explained that a French explorer and missionary named Pére Amide had come here in the seventeenth century to trade pelts and convert the natives into Christians. Somehow his name had been rolled into Pyramid.

We headed down Main Street, and there was everything we needed: Buzz's Diner, Suomi's Quick Stop and Gas Station, Amide's Coffee Shop, and the By Gone Consignment Boutique. There was even a health food store down on South Main.

The Pyramid Motel was closed, its windows smashed, but a newly opened Best Western offered $99 suites with

Jacuzzi. We pulled into the parking lot, and Ma went inside to get us a room for the night.

I stepped out of the car to stretch my legs. It was the beginning of April, and there was only a touch of spring in the air. There would be no sticky summer heat here like in Georgia. This far north the sky was darker blue, the clouds faster moving.

Dad was from Minnesota, I thought, looking around. *He might have liked it here, too.*

* * *

The next day was Monday. Ma found work at the Golden Acres Retirement Home, and we moved into #8C, third floor, Century Terrace Apartments. It was the beginning of spring break, so school wasn't back in session yet, and I spent the day alone. I worried that Ma would soon be with another Mr. Someone. I knew I couldn't really prevent that, but during the long hours in the Volvo, I had come up with a plan — I wanted us to buy a house.

Back in Georgia, before we'd moved into our house in Marietta, I remembered Ma and Dad talking about coming up with the down payment and paying a mortgage instead of rent. Ma had done the math and said it would be cheaper in the long run to own a house. Dad had expressed some doubts and called it a "serious commitment," but in the end, he had agreed to it.

That was exactly what I needed now. I needed Ma to commit to Pyramid by buying a house.

At the health food store I found a brochure with real estate listings. But when I brought it home and showed it to Ma that evening, she didn't seem interested.

"I think we should look for a house and put down some money," I said while she was getting ready for her new evening job at the diner.

"Truth be told, I don't even know if I want to stay here," Ma said.

"What do you mean?" I asked.

She shrugged. "There might be a better place out there."

"Pyramid is as good a place as any," I argued. "You've already got two jobs. And there's a middle school here. Spring break will be over soon. You could register me tomorrow."

"They have snow here from October to May."

"I don't mind snow. I don't want to move around anymore," I said. "And I'm looking for a job to add money to our savings account. I asked at the health food store and —"

"We're nowhere close to having enough money for a down payment on a house, even if you did get a job, Wren," Ma interrupted.

"We have three thousand four hundred and thirty dollars in the savings account," I told her. "I saw the statements you withdrew from the ATM in Ohio."

"That's barely enough for the closing costs."

Anticipating trouble, I had looked this up at the library earlier and done the math. I'd asked the librarian and learned that the minimum we needed to put down was five percent. My plan was to find a decent house we could afford and make Ma sign the mortgage papers before she could start dating again.

"It'll put us only about five hundred and seventy dollars short of what we need for a down payment," I explained. "We could get a decent two-bedroom one-bath house here for about eighty thousand dollars."

Ma ignored me, looking through her purse for her car keys.

"I think Dad might have liked it here," I continued. "He used to tell me the sky in Min—"

"You know that I don't want to talk about your dad," Ma interrupted with a warning look.

"Why can't we talk about him?" I whined, hating my teary voice.

"There's nothing to talk about."

"But . . ." I couldn't finish. The cloud crushed what I wanted to say, and I could feel tears welling up in my throat. I didn't want to cry.

Ma sighed. "We've been through this."

"I miss him. You must miss him too." I choked up. "I miss him every day. Don't you . . ." I couldn't say any more.

Ma took a deep breath and picked up her jacket. "I have to go to work." She left without even turning around.

That's when I made a decision. Ma might not ever want to talk to me about my dead father, but I didn't want us to continue hopping from place to place. I was determined to make my plan work.

I took the map of Michigan from my bag, drew a red arrow pointing directly at Pyramid, and taped it on the refrigerator door. Then I circled Pyramid.

This was where our journey would end.

8

I swear the crow wanted me to find the pond.

The day after we moved into the apartment, I went out on my bike early in the morning. It was still spring break in Pyramid, so I had lots of time to explore while Ma was at work. Passing a stretch of forest, I had trouble with my front tire and got off to check if it needed air. That's when a crow landed in a tree next to me, drawing attention to itself with loud caws. It had a tiny white spot between its beak and right eye. After making quite a racket, it flew off, swooped around in a tight curve, and landed right back on the same branch.

My tire was fine. I stood and looked at the noisy bird. It appeared to be studying me. I thought of Dad and how he would have said, "She's watching you, Wren." It really did seem that way. Every time our eyes met, the crow let out a deep caw and started another swoop, as if saying, "Follow me."

I dropped my bicycle in the grass and followed the crow into the forest. For a while, we played a game of hide-and-seek. When I pulled out my binoculars, it flew off with shrill calls. That's how I discovered the pond.

It was a magical place. I felt it right away. Fog steamed up from the water, and trunks of dead birch trees formed a half circle around the opposite shore. There was no human sound, just birdsongs and the swampy smell of wet earth. I sat down on a flat boulder in the reeds and listened to the birds.

I didn't know if I could bird-watch again — not without Dad. But then I saw a sparrow landing in a tree next to the boulder and let my eyes follow it. You have to concentrate to watch birds, but it's fun to try and identify the kind of bird you're looking at. Dad and I had always shared that fun.

I waited for the cloud to smother me in the kind of pain that would tell me that I could never watch birds again. But it didn't come. Instead, I registered the bird's characteristics.

"Look for size, color, song," Dad used to say. "You'll learn to tell them apart."

This one had a streaked body and a dark tail with white edges. I recognized it by its song: four notes — the last two higher — followed by a descending series of trills. Dad had said it sounded like, "Where-where-come-come-all-together-down-the-hill."

When I got home, I checked in my bird book. *Vesper Sparrow: Often sings in the evening twilight.*

For the first time since Dad's death, I opened my bird journal to note my sighting. Printed on the first page was a quote.

" . . . *be light like a bird, and not like a feather.*"

— *Paul Valéry*

When Dad had given the journal to me, I'd asked him what that meant. He'd said, "It means you don't want to just float around in life like a feather. You want to determine your own direction — fly and soar like a bird."

At the time, I'd thought Dad would help me find that direction. Now it made me sad to think of our conversation. I certainly didn't feel like I was flying like a bird, full of intention and self-direction.

I filled in the date, location, time, and weather. Below my notes, I tried to draw an outline of the sparrow. It looked like a crooked egg with a tail. I couldn't even copy it from the book. I erased it, tried again, and then gave up. Dad had always been the better drawer. He'd told me I'd get better if I kept trying. I knew then that he would have wanted me to continue bird-watching.

* * *

The next time I went back to the pond, a crow once again sat on the stump. I took out my binoculars for a closer look. I saw the tiny white spot on its face and knew it was the same bird that had led me there before.

I went back every day that week, bringing nuts with me for the crow. I threw them under the tree he usually perched on, but he didn't touch them while I was there. He waited until I walked to the other side of the pond, and when I came back, the nuts were gone. I had no idea if the bird was a female or a male, but I called him Joseph, after St. Joseph of Cupertino — the patron saint of pilots.

9

As I entered Eats of Eden, Mr. Leroy, the owner of the health food store, greeted me with a cheerful, *"Bon Jour. Comment ça va?"*

"Pas mal," I answered, which means *not bad.*

Mr. Leroy was French. That's why his name was pronounced *Lee-rwah.* Most people said *Lee-roi* instead. But at least he had a good sense of humor about it. He'd told me when he hired me that he was glad that his name wasn't Monsieur Bouchard, which would have sounded like "butchered" in America.

Not much taller than me and a bit pudgy around his middle, Mr. Leroy wore his gray hair slicked back so you could see his widow's peak. His dark blue eyes were hidden behind horn-rimmed Harry Potter glasses. If I hadn't known better, I'd have thought he sold used books.

"Any deliveries?" I asked as I took off my jacket.

"No," he replied. "It's been a quiet day."

So far it seemed like most days here were quiet. I'd asked Mr. Leroy if he needed help when I'd gone exploring the day after we arrived in Pyramid, and he'd hired me right away. After spring break was over I wouldn't be able to come more than once a week, but judging from the low customer volume I'd observed, I assumed Mr. Leroy had other sources of income to stay afloat. I wondered if he only hired me for company. In any case, the money I would earn in the store would go right into our down payment fund.

"Assam? Or Darjeeling?" Mr. Leroy asked. He was a tea fanatic — a *connoisseur*, as he called himself.

"You choose," I said, sitting down behind the counter to watch him fuss with the tea.

"I circled a listing for you," he said, motioning toward the newspaper on the counter. Mr. Leroy didn't know about Dad. I'd only told him that I lived with my mother in an apartment and that I was hoping we would move into a small house soon.

"Two bedrooms, one bath, large porch, located on Cedar Drive. Perfect starter home," I read aloud.

"Cedar Drive is a decent address," Mr. Leroy said.

"And it's less than eighty thousand, which is our limit," I said. "Can I take this page?"

Mr. Leroy nodded, and I ripped out the page and stuffed it into my pocket. As he served our tea, I studied his hands. I assumed he wasn't married since he didn't wear a wedding ring and had never mentioned a woman in his life.

"Have you ever been married, Mr. Leroy?" I asked after we'd finished our tea and were unpacking chia seed and quinoa boxes. He was standing on top of the ladder while I was handing him packets.

"I have been," he said.

"And why are you not anymore?"

"We got divorced," he said. "Teresa and I were married for six years." He placed the last package on the shelf and stepped down from the ladder. "And now do you want to know why we separated?"

"I do."

"She fell in love with another man."

I frowned. "That must have hurt."

"It sure did," he said.

"How did you get over it?" I asked.

"Time."

"How much time?"

"Oh, it takes a while," Mr. Leroy said. "And the healing doesn't go in a straight line from feeling bad to feeling better. It's more like a zigzag." He drew an imaginary zigzag line in the air. "Some days you think you are better, and then, a few days later, you feel terrible again."

"Have you met another woman since your divorce?" I asked.

"No," he said, shaking his head. "I think that chapter in my life is closed."

I nodded. It sounded kind of sad. I didn't want to pry anymore.

Just then a young woman entered the store. While Mr. Leroy went up front to ring her up, I went back to the counter and skimmed the headlines in the paper. On page two, I found an article entitled "Planned Expansion of the Pyramid Landfill." It read:

> . . . more space needed to accommodate higher waste volume . . . planned extension will incorporate the swamp area known as Pete's Pond . . . an environmental impact study gave the green light . . . expected that the motion will have smooth sailing in the council . . . area is currently being surveyed in preparation for the fence installation . . .

Mr. Leroy returned to the back of the store just as I was finishing the article.

"Did you know they're planning to destroy someplace called Pete's Pond?" I said. "I think I've been there and watched birds. It's beautiful. The paper says they've already started surveying the area before the township board has even voted on it."

He shook his head. "That's no surprise to me."

"But how can they do that?"

"The board is in the hands of a few influential locals who pretty much wheel and deal everything among themselves. The owner of the landfill is even one of the board's trustees. Something like this is already a *fait accompli.*"

There was my word of the day. When I'd first visited the store, I had asked Mr. Leroy to teach me a few French words, and he thought it would be good if I memorized a word a day once I started working there. So I pulled out my notebook and handed it to him.

Mr. Leroy wrote *fait accompli* in his lovely French cursive on one side of the page and handed it back to me. Next to it I noted the definition he gave me: *Irreversible action that has happened before those affected know of its existence*, or *a done deal*.

* * *

On my way home, I stopped at the pond. When I took my seat on the boulder, I saw a flock of female turkeys coming out of the underbrush. After a few steps, one of the hens stopped and looked around nervously while the others continued. I wondered if it was hard for a girl turkey to make friends or if it just came naturally to them to stick together. Maybe their gurgling sound was actually a turkey giggle, and while they made fun of one of the other hens, she only pretended to be laughing too.

Suddenly, there was movement among the dead trees across the pond. A man in an orange safety vest bent over a telescope on a yellow tripod. Then branches snapped behind me. Another man in a similar vest stepped out from the bushes, holding a long pole painted in broad red-and-white stripes.

"What's that for?" I asked.

"We're marking the borders to prepare it for clearing," he explained.

"Clearing?" I repeated.

The man shrugged. "I guess they'll cut everything down and drain the pond. As soon as we're done, the bulldozers will come."

Just then a shrill cackle shot from the walkie-talkie in his vest pocket. "You're off, Bob," a distorted voice squeaked through the small black box. "You need to move about three meters to your right."

The surveyor held the walkie-talkie close to his mouth to answer. "Sorry, Landon. I'm moving right now." He turned to me. "I've got to get back to work. Nice meeting you."

"Bye." I nodded, watching the man disappear from view.

Cleared by bulldozers? I thought. I imagined men cutting down trees, the sound of their chainsaws driving away the birds, destroying my place.

I stood up to leave. I was done with birding for today, too upset to stay.

10

I would be the new girl in school again. The week of spring break had ended in Pyramid, and I had joined Chippewa County Middle School, a flat brown building on the outskirts of Sault Ste. Marie. On my way to school the first day I realized that if this was the place I wanted us to stay, I would have to fit in somehow.

I got lucky.

The first day, I sat next to Carrie, one of the popular girls in school, and let her copy the answers to the math worksheet. I knew this was my chance. I wouldn't be a loner if I could hang out with Carrie. Her paying attention to me was like an oversized thousand-watt stadium light had suddenly focused on me. In her spotlight, I almost felt like I gave off light myself.

But to attract Carrie's light, I had to get to school early so she could copy my homework. Only a week after my first day, as I pushed my way through the stampede of students, craning my head to scan the hall for Carrie's beautiful hair, I saw her standing by the vending machine, talking to a girl I didn't recognize.

"Meet Victoria," Carrie said when I approached. "She'll be in our class. It's her first day."

Victoria had an angel face framed by the kind of golden curls I'd always wanted. My hair, on the other hand, was thin, cropped short, and the color of whole wheat bread.

"This is Wren!" Carrie added.

A sting. She hadn't said, "*my friend* Wren."

"Victoria just moved here from Ann Arbor," Carrie explained. And there was more. "Victoria's mom is a yoga instructor. My mom already met her. She wants to take her class at the community college!"

"Maybe your mom would also like to sign up," Victoria said to me.

I shook my head. "My mother works different shifts, and they change all the time." Lack of time wasn't the only reason Ma wouldn't sign up for a yoga class, but I didn't want to tell them that we also didn't have money to spend on yoga classes. I took my math notebook out of my backpack and handed it to Carrie.

"Wren is really good at math," Carrie explained.

An awkward silence followed as Victoria and I both watched Carrie scribble my answers in her notebook. When she was done, Victoria pointed to a photo of a dumb boy band that was glued to Carrie's notebook cover.

"I *love* the Silver Pears!" She practically screamed the word *love*, nodding frantically, her golden curls bouncing on her shoulders.

I looked for dandruff, but there was nothing. If something were to fall out of Victoria's hair, it would probably be gold dust. I could already feel my light dimming.

* * *

The Carrie-Victoria lovefest continued.

Our homeroom teacher, Mrs. Anderson was also delighted to meet Victoria. "Who'd like to be the new girl's buddy?" she asked.

Carrie beamed. "I'm happy to show her around!"

Another sting. Just a week ago, when I'd been the new girl, Carrie hadn't volunteered to be my guide. She'd only warmed to me after I'd helped her with a math test.

When we entered social studies class Mrs. Peters had changed the seating arrangement. The desks in our classroom were now arranged in groups of four, and she had placed name cards on each table. Carrie and I would sit with a quiet, nerdy boy named Theo. One desk in our group was empty, and I knew what was coming.

Mrs. Peters pointed to the empty chair opposite Carrie. "Perfect. Victoria can join your group."

A minute later Theo entered the classroom, looking like he had stepped out of an old black-and-white movie. He was dressed in a flannel shirt and corduroy pants, and his hair was parted straight and slicked back from his forehead in a roll. The rectangular black frames of his glasses seemed too big for his face. I'd once seen a boy in an old milk advertisement with hair like that, and I could have sworn he and Theo were wearing the same shirt.

Theo took his seat at our table. Victoria turned to Carrie, mouthing the word *nerd* to confirm her first impression. Carrie rolled her eyes in agreement.

"Good morning, boys and girls!" Mrs. Peters said. She was ready to begin the day with a civics unit. "Who remembers the definition of a controversy?"

Theo's hand shot up. "A controversy is a dispute or disagreement between sides holding opposite views," he said in his earnest voice.

I sighed. What a toxic thing to say! In the group behind me, Tim and Callum groaned softly.

"Very good, Theo," Mrs. Peters said. "Controversial public policy issues are often framed by *should* questions. Such as, *'Should we share the water of the Great Lakes with desert states?'* Or, *'Should we lower the voting age?'*"

Callum whispered, "Should Theo get a new haircut?" The kids in his group chuckled. I could see in Theo's eyes that he'd heard Callum's remark.

"Our next assignment will be a partner project," Mrs. Peters continued. "Each group will choose one controversial issue, find out the facts, as well as the pros and cons, and then argue for one side or the other."

Everyone in the class quickly sought to make eye contact with their preferred partner. I looked over to Carrie, but her eyes were locked onto Victoria's.

"I will assign the partners," Mrs. Peters said as she handed out the papers.

Last week partners had been assigned randomly, with the help of the *sticks of doom* — Popsicle sticks that had our names written on them in black marker. Mrs. Peters would close her eyes and pull out two sticks, then read the names aloud, and that was that. It seemed fair to me. At least chance determined whom you had to work with. But this time Mrs. Peters announced that we'd be working with someone at our table. As she went around the room assigning team partners, I held my breath and squeezed my thumbs inside my fists, hoping for a miracle.

"Carrie, why don't you work with Victoria?" Mrs. Peters said when she got to our table. "And Theo can work with Wren."

I looked down to the stone-gray linoleum tiles, hiding my disappointment. Carrie and Victoria would bond over their work while I had to spend time with Theo the nerd. The light Carrie had shone on me went from dim to extinguished.

When I looked back up, my eyes met Theo's. He looked at me apologetically, as if it were his fault that I'd ended up with him. I glared at him. I wanted him to feel bad, too.

On the board, Mrs. Peters made a list of possible report topics:

- Should power be generated from coal or nuclear energy?

- Should Michigan share the water of the Great Lakes with other states?

- Should voting be mandatory? Who cares?

Carrie and Victoria picked their topic right away, eager to work together.

Theo turned to me. "Which one do you want to do?"

I shrugged, thinking, *I don't want to work on any of them with you.*

Mrs. Peters was standing next to our desks. "How about, *'Should seat belts be mandatory on school buses?'*" she suggested in a cheerful voice.

"I don't take the school bus. I ride my bike to school," I said.

"Me too," Theo agreed with a nod.

"There are also local topics," Mrs. Peters said. "I read in the paper that the township plans to expand the landfill."

"They've already started to survey the area," I blurted out. "I saw it. It's so sad!"

"There's nothing wrong with it," Carrie piped up. "My dad runs the landfill. They just need more space."

I frowned. *Why did I not know that about her?*

"Who cares about that swamp anyway?" Carrie added.

"Pete's Pond is not just a swamp," I said quietly. In my mind I added, *There's actually a wetland surrounding the pond with very exciting birdlife.*

"Sounds like this is already controversial here in our classroom," Mrs. Peters said with an encouraging smile. "Theo, what do you think?"

Theo was the master of pauses. He didn't seem to mind that a gigantic silence spread out, hovering in the middle of the conversation. He just sat there, thinking about an answer. "I wonder why we need that space to bury garbage," he finally said. "The town hasn't grown very much."

Mrs. Peters gave us a big smile. "Looks like you've already figured out why this is an interesting issue." She wrote our names and the topic on her chart.

After school Carrie and Victoria left the building together, giggling as if they had known each other forever, just like a pair of turkey hens.

11

After school Theo waited for me at the bike racks. He wanted to check out Pete's Pond. I could hardly say no since we were working on this project together. But I made sure he was out of breath by the time we got there. After we parked our bikes, we walked around the pond, and I showed him the landfill behind the trees to the east.

"You see," I said, when we returned to our bikes, "it's not just a pond. It's more a kind of wetland with lots of birds."

"How come you know this area so well?" Theo asked, his face flushed and his cowlick now dissolved into wisps.

"Sometimes I come here when I want to be alone," I said vaguely. He didn't need to know what the place meant to me.

"All of this is going to be a big garbage dump," he said. "That's kind of sad."

"*Kind* of sad? That's not what I'd call it," I snapped. "I'd say it's a terrible, awful destruction of nature. Tragic, really." I glared at him as if it was all his fault and pushed my bike closer to the road. The cloud was throwing a dark shadow over me. I needed to leave.

Before I could get away, Theo said, "I know you don't want to work with me. So let's get it over with quickly."

"It's not like that —" I started, but he wouldn't let me finish.

"You don't have to explain," he said calmly. "You wanted to work with Carrie, but she preferred Victoria."

"I'm sorry, I . . ."

"No need to be sorry," Theo said. "Let's just work swiftly to get it over with."

I couldn't look at him.

"Mrs. Peters recommended that we start with a list of questions," he continued. "The public library is closed today, but we can go to my house and work there."

After what he'd just said about me not wanting to work with him, I couldn't say no. So I nodded and followed him on my bike.

* * *

Theo's home was an older house. The dark gray paint was flaking off around the eaves and windows, and the lawn needed cutting. When I stepped on the middle stair of the porch, a board popped up. I almost stumbled.

"My dad will fix that this weekend," Theo said, opening the screen door with a creak.

I followed him into the house. Inside, it smelled like old garbage. I'd heard a rumor at school that Theo lived with just his dad, but I wouldn't bring it up. I didn't want to give him the impression that we had something in common.

On the way to the staircase, we passed a room filled with bookcases and a leather chair next to a reading lamp.

"Wow," I said. "You guys have a lot of books."

"My dad likes to read," Theo said, sliding his hand up and down on the banister.

"What does he do?"

"He teaches history at the university."

"That must be interesting," I said.

Theo shrugged. "I wish he was more interested in practical things."

I followed Theo upstairs. For a boy, his room was tidy. The bed was made properly, and a row of shoes was lined against the closet door.

Without another word, Theo opened his computer, and we got to work. It was actually easy to work with him. We came up with good questions without any arguing, and he quickly typed them up. When I'd worked on a science experiment with Carrie last week, she'd let me do all the work alone. I hadn't really minded, but working with Theo made me realize how different it was when you truly shared a project with someone.

I didn't want to make it look like I was in a hurry to leave after we were done with our list of questions, so instead I pointed to the shelf near his bed, which held several large photo albums and several cameras. "What kind of pictures do you take?" I asked.

"I take photos of all kinds of things," Theo said hesitantly. "Mostly objects that don't move."

"Like what? Trees? Houses?"

"Not really," he said. "You want to see some?"

I nodded, and Theo opened one of the albums to a photo of different-colored gummy bears arranged in ten rows of ten.

"It's an array of one-hundred gummy bears," he said. "I did one with peanuts, too." He pulled the album onto his lap and searched through it. "Here!" He pointed to a photo of five rows of five peanuts on a checkered background. "I'm working on an array of screws."

While I studied the image, I searched my head for something to say. There was nothing wrong with taking such photos. The items, set against contrasting backgrounds, made you look at them in a different way. It was a little weird, maybe, but kind of artsy.

"I think they're kind of artsy," I finally said.

Theo gave me a small smile. He seemed to like hearing that.

I opened a page toward the end of the album. There was a black-and-white photo of a dead raccoon. Its tail and lower body were squashed onto the pavement. A bloodstain spread like a dark aura around the furry body.

I swallowed and didn't look at him when I asked, "Why do you take pictures of dead animals?"

"I used to be attracted to sad things," Theo said quietly. I could tell he would have rather not shown that photo to me. "I bet you find that kind of weird."

"No, no," I said, rubbing my hands on the sides of my jeans.

"I can show you some other photos."

"It's okay. I have to go now," I said, wishing I hadn't seen the picture of the dead raccoon.

I used to be attracted to sad things. Theo's words echoed in my head as I hurried toward the door.

12

The next day as we were walking out for recess, Victoria held up a glossy magazine. "My mother bought me a *Miss Magazine*." She pointed to the photo of a girl in a pink dress on the cover. "Isn't she just gorgeous?"

I glanced briefly at the photo before my eyes wandered to a pair of robins chasing each other on the other side of the schoolyard. I didn't care for *Miss Magazine*, but I was afraid I'd have to fake interest if I wanted to fit in with Carrie and Victoria.

"This issue has a quiz," Victoria continued. "'Are You and Your Friend Compatible?'"

"Let's do it," Carrie said. "I have a pen."

Victoria adjusted the magazine on her lap. "What's your favorite food?" she asked Carrie as she read.

"Fish fingers!"

Victoria sighed. "Mine is pizza. I wish it wasn't so fattening."

"Uhh! Bad girl!" Carrie scolded.

"How about you?" Victoria asked. They both looked at me.

"Pizza," I said.

"What's your favorite animal?" Victoria asked, focusing on Carrie again.

"Poodle!" Carrie squeaked. "I hope I get one for my birthday! My dad wants me to volunteer at the shelter first to prove that I really know how to take care of a dog." She rolled her eyes. "Do you want to come with me?"

Victoria shook her head. "I'm allergic to dog hair."

"That's okay," Carrie said quickly. "You can still come visit even if I do get a poodle. They don't shed."

"I'll go with you to the shelter," I offered. "I like dogs."

"Okay," Carrie said, shrugging. "I'll have to go next Thursday."

"Let's continue with the quiz," Victoria said. "How about your favorite color?" She turned to Carrie, and in unison they both yelled: "Pink!" before breaking out in hysterical laughter.

"Green. I love all shades of green," I said.

"Next question," Victoria said. "If you had to spend a week on a deserted island and could only take three things, what would you take?"

"That's easy," Carrie said. "I'd take my gel pens, my journal, my pink sweater."

"I'd take my photo album, my favorite quilt, and my pink jacket," Victoria said.

If I had to spend a week on a deserted island, I would take matches so I could make a fire. I'd take my binoculars to observe birds or watch for a boat to come. I'd also need a pocketknife. But I knew I couldn't say what I really thought.

"I would take . . ." I began slowly.

But Victoria was already reading the next question. She looked at me, and when I didn't finish my sentence she said, "Okay, you can come back to that one." Then she read the last question: "What is your favorite hobby?"

Carrie spit out her answer. "Playing tennis."

Victoria nodded eagerly. "Mine is playing tennis too!"

They both looked at me. "What's yours?"

I didn't want them to roll their eyes when I said I liked watching birds. Maybe I should tell them I liked to read. That was also true and much safer. But before I could give an answer, the bell rang, and I was glad we had to go back to class. It was easier to avoid answering than be true to myself.

13

Theo and I agreed to do our research in the public library right after school. "It's quieter there, and Mrs. Russo, the librarian, is way nicer than our school's librarian," Theo told me after class. "I'll introduce you to her."

He was right. Mrs. Russo was nice. I liked the way her gray hair was cropped so short that it looked like a bath cap. She wore a purple turtleneck without any jewelry or makeup. And her office smelled like sandalwood.

"Welcome to Pyramid," Mrs. Russo said after Theo introduced me. She took off her reading glasses and gave me a firm handshake.

Theo explained our project, and Mrs. Russo told us she thought we'd picked an "awesome topic." She helped us find books we could use for research, and we settled in at the oblong table in the back of the reading room. My task was to find out about the landfill's history, while Theo checked on environmental protection regulations.

After a while I zoned out and stared at the magazine rack next to the window. On the glossy cover of *Aviator*, a jet like the one Dad used to fly hung suspended in midair over some snowy mountain peaks. In my mind, the jet began to move and gain altitude.

"Wren? Are you listening?" Theo looked at me across the table, with the book *Garbage and You* in his hands.

I turned away from the magazine and refocused on Theo. "Sorry, what'd you say?"

"In 2013, Americans generated about two hundred and fifty-four million tons of trash," Theo said. "Imagine!"

"Hmm, that's a lot of garbage," I replied.

"It says here that Americans composted and recycled eighty-seven million tons of trash," Theo continued. "That's a recycling rate of about thirty-four percent. Did you know that recycling rates in Austria and Germany are much higher?"

I nodded.

"You did?" he asked. "I had no idea."

"No, sorry, I didn't either," I said, shaking my head. "I wasn't listening." I looked back down at my book and tried to refocus on my reading, but I had to get up. I couldn't concentrate. "I think I'll do some research online."

"Maybe you could add something to the report about why other countries have higher recycling rates," Theo suggested. "They might not need to destroy wetlands to expand landfills."

I nodded and walked over to the library computers, sitting down in front of one. But when the browser opened, I typed the words *remains of plane crash victims*. A list of links appeared on the screen. I clicked on one and read:

. . . results from a 2008 study published in the magazine Forensic Science . . . *different conditions of remains retrieved from airplanes crashes . . . One victim, found off Sicily a month after death, was still fully dressed. A three-month-old body discovered off the coast of Africa had been fully skeletonized by flesh-eating shrimp-like creatures.*

The words expanded under the cloud. I imagined Dad's body on the ocean floor . . . skeletonized by flesh-eating shrimp.

"What are you doing?"

I heard Theo behind me, and quickly closed the site. "Sorry," I said, feeling myself blush. "I'm distracted." I was glad I was facing the computer screen so he couldn't see my red face.

"How's your research coming along?" Mrs. Russo asked, walking into the reading room.

Theo threw me a long look before he gave her a short summary of what he'd learned, making it sound like we had done it together. I was glad that Theo had covered for me. But I couldn't let him do all of the work by himself. I needed to contribute something. And to do that, I needed to get out from under the cloud.

14

The next day after school, Theo and I rode our bikes to the landfill. On the way, I reminded myself that I had to concentrate more on our project. Things couldn't go on as they had the day before in the library.

Mr. Zusack — Carrie's dad and the owner of the landfill — had an office in the back room of an uninspired-looking flat-roofed building to the right of the entrance gate. We locked our bikes to a chain-link fence and told his secretary that he would be expecting us.

"Welcome to the Pyramid Landfill," Mr. Zusack said, motioning for us to come closer to a map hanging on his office wall. "Carrie told me about your school project. I have to say, I'm a little surprised you chose this topic since there's actually nothing controversial going on. But I'm happy to tell you about the landfill."

He started talking, but again I couldn't focus. All I could think was that Mr. Zusack should buy bigger shirts. His belly pressed against the buttons, and his fleshy arms stretched the fabric of his shirt like sausage casings. At one point I caught him using the words *sanitary landfill,* and I couldn't help but think of a sanitary napkin.

With a big false smile on his face, Mr. Zusack added, "That means we can only store nontoxic waste such as household garbage."

While he continued talking about daily volume, excavation lining, and gas release, I stared out the big window. In the distance, a man stopped his car near the rim of a low excavation filled with garbage. He pulled a carpet roll out of his trunk and threw it on top of a heap of other large items. It joined a jumble of shelves, sofa pillows, and a mattress with its springs exposed, in this junkyard cemetery.

"Why don't you recycle?" Theo asked.

"There hasn't been enough interest," Mr. Zusack said.

"Did you know that in Austria the recycling rate is more than sixty percent, while in the United States we only recycle about thirty-five percent of our trash?" Theo asked.

Mr. Zusack shrugged. "They do a lot of things differently over there."

"Don't you feel bad about destroying the wetland?" I asked.

"It's a business, Wren," Mr. Zusack said. I really didn't like the condescending tone in his voice. "People need a place to drop their waste, and I provide that for them." Then his face broke out into a shark-like smile, and he added, "It's all about supply and demand."

He made it sound totally logical that he had to destroy the wetland so more people could throw carpets into a big ditch.

Just then the door opened, and the sheriff's massive body filled the frame. "Howdy," he said, lifting his hat. "Has my brother here told you how to turn trash into gold? That's what he does here, kids!" A deep laugh bounced the belly under his shirt.

I caught Theo's glance and knew we were both thinking the same thing: *The sheriff and Mr. Zusack are brothers?*

* * *

We didn't stay much longer, and when we were back outside, I shuddered. "I don't like Mr. Zusack," I said. "He talked to us like we were in kindergarten. And I can't believe the sheriff is his brother."

"It's no surprise that the men who have influence in this town are sticking together. My dad calls them a 'ruling clique,'" Theo said.

"Did you tell your dad about the landfill and our project?" I asked.

"No," Theo said, "but my dad is interested in politics. Or at least he used to be. A long time ago, before we moved here, he was even a city councilman."

"But he's not in politics anymore?" I asked.

Theo shook his head. "Since my mother died he hasn't shown interest in anything."

"Your mother died?" I said. "When?"

"Two years ago," Theo replied. "She had cancer."

"I'm sorry."

That's all I could say. It made me uncomfortable that Theo had told me about his mother. He shouldn't be so open with me. That was something you shouldn't share with anyone unless you really liked and trusted that person. Didn't he realize that I could never be his friend? Sure, we had things in common, but an interest in roadkill and a dead parent were the wrong things. Being with someone as sad and lonely as Theo would only make my loneliness worse. I didn't want to know why he took photos of roadkill, and I wasn't about to ask him about his mother.

15

Carrie caught up with me after social studies class the next day. "I'm sorry you ended up with Theo," she said as she checked her reflection in the glass door leading to the janitor's office.

"It's okay," I said. "He knows a lot, so the work is easier."

Carrie shrugged. "That's the good thing, I guess. But he's such a nerd. Does he ever laugh?"

"Yeah, he does," I said. "He's just different."

"Who are you talking about?" Victoria asked as she joined us, her hair tied into a voluminous ponytail.

"We're talking about Theo," Carrie said. "Poor Wren has to work with him on the report."

"Yeah, poor you!" Victoria turned to me, all fake concern. "Where does he get those shirts?"

"His mother must alter the ones she got from her grandfather," Victoria said, bursting out in shrill laughter. Carrie laughed too. I did not.

"And the hair!" Victoria continued. "He probably parts it every morning with a ruler."

I moved my facial muscles into what I hoped looked like a smile, but the laughter stuck in my throat. "He's not that bad," I said. "He's really smart. I think he's just lonely."

As if on cue, Carrie and Victoria stopped their laughter and turned to me in mock surprise, eyebrows raised. For a second, I envisioned a miniature version of myself crawling inside one of the lockers next to us and closing the door behind me.

Carrie said, "Someone likes someone here, Wren?" She stretched my name into one long "nnnnnnn," lifting her head, as if pulling me up on that one letter.

I shook my head. "Noooo!" It sounded weak.

Victoria broke out into a singsong, "Wren likes Theo. Wren likes Theo. Wren likes . . ." She looked at Carrie to join in the chorus.

I knew I was supposed to laugh and make some crazy gesture, like covering my ears with my hands, or shaking my head wildly, or throwing my hands up in the air in protest. But my brain switched into slow motion. I couldn't lift my arms to perform one of the required exaggerated gestures; instead I just waited for them to leave.

* * *

In the back room of the health food store, where Mr. Leroy did all of his paperwork, hung a framed postcard with a black-and-white photograph of an old Frenchman holding a pipe. He had slick dark hair and the same kind of horn-rimmed glasses Mr. Leroy wore. Mr. Leroy had told me the man was a famous French philosopher named Jean-Paul Sartre. On the bottom of the card, one of his famous sayings was printed in bold letters: *L'enfer c'est les autres.*

When I'd asked about the postcard, Mr. Leroy had given me the translation. I'd copied the quote right into my notebook where I collected all the French words he'd taught me. It meant: *Hell is other people.*

I couldn't agree more.

16

For the rest of the afternoon I kept replaying the scene in my head. First I got angry with Victoria and Carrie for teasing me. Then I got angry with myself for not standing up to them. Then I got even angrier with myself for letting this bother me so much. By the end of last period I was in a royally bad mood.

After school I jumped on my bike and raced over to Pete's Pond. I hurried through the woods, longing for the moment the water would come into view.

Only a few steps away from the long grass encircling the pond, I slowed down. Someone was sitting on my boulder. I recognized the jacket — Theo. He was following a crow with his camera as it flew across the water.

"What are *you* doing here?" My voice sounded shrill.

Theo jerked his head around and looked at me, startled. "I'm watching birds and taking pictures of them."

"You can't be here! This is my place!"

One of Theo's long pauses hung in the air. Joseph, the crow, landed in the tree next to us.

"That can't be true," Theo said calmly. "We wrote in our report that Pete's Pond is public land. It doesn't belong to you."

"You know what I mean," I snapped. "I need to have this place for myself!"

Why do I sound like a five-year-old throwing a tantrum?

"But . . ." Theo began.

"Don't you have a dead raccoon to take a picture of?" I glared at him.

Something in Theo's face shifted, and he suddenly looked sad.

I felt the taste of tears welling up in my throat. I looked at Joseph. The bird cocked his head and let out a caw. Then he flew off.

Theo got up and walked away.

* * *

I climbed up on the boulder. I'd had no choice but to do that. It was better that Theo didn't hang out here. This was my place, and I couldn't share bird-watching with him. No way.

I tried concentrating on a pair of black-capped chickadees, but I kept thinking of the way Theo had looked at me before he left. I shouldn't have done what I did. I'd been mean to him — unnecessarily mean.

A moment later I gave up. I couldn't focus on birds anymore and walked back to my bike to ride home.

On 6 Mile Road I saw a dead squirrel. I got off, put my bike in the grass, and took out my trowel to dig a hole. The hit-and-run must have occurred some time ago. There was already that nauseatingly sweet smell of decomposing flesh, and a car had run over the lower part of the body. It looked like a bird had pulled its innards out, but had been interrupted. Flies buzzed on a mass of dark red tissue attached to what appeared to be a blood vessel or a piece of intestine draped in a perfect crescent around the carcass.

A ray of sunlight suddenly illuminated the bloody mess, and for a moment it almost looked like a striking piece of art. I thought of Theo and how this would have made an unusual photo. I hated myself for being mean to him.

After I was done, I sat next to the small grave and waited to see if the burial would bring me some relief, would make me feel less rotten. It didn't. The cloud pressed down, heavier than ever.

A car stopped, and a woman asked if I was okay. I put on a smile and lied.

17

"I filled out the form for the post office so they can forward our mail to our new address," I said later that night as I watched Ma make dinner. "All you have to do is sign it."

"We don't really have to do that," Ma said, still facing the stove. "It'll just flood our mailbox with ads."

"What if they find something from the crash?" I said. "They'll need to know how to contact us."

Ma turned around, and for a second I thought I saw a flicker in her eyes. Then she asked, "How do you like my new hairdo?"

I studied her a moment. Light streaks were scattered through her hair. It had been cut shorter and blow-dried to a swift roll, framing her chin on both sides. The new hairdo brought out her eyes more, but I didn't want to tell her that.

"Seems longer on one side," I said instead.

Ma stepped over to the mirror to check. "I don't think so," she said, cupping the inward rolls with both hands.

I frowned. Ma didn't need to be more attractive. She already had a perfect figure and flawless skin. Even if she threw on her old rain jacket with the ripped sleeve, she couldn't go to the gas station without several men ogling her. I hadn't gotten any of her beauty; I looked gangly and plain like Dad.

Ma finished admiring herself and turned back to the stove, stirring the red contents of a can into a pot.

"New color and streaks plus cut. That must have been expensive," I said.

Ma shrugged. "A hundred dollars including tip. Something wrong with that?"

"We need money for our down payment," I said.

"We aren't even close to having enough money to buy a house." Ma let out a sigh and gave the red mass in the pot a stir. "But I'm working extra shifts at the diner.

You should be happy; attractive waitresses get better tips." She winked at me and added, "Call it a return on my investment."

I didn't like the sassy way she said that. There could also be another kind of return. The kind where she attracted another man and started dating again.

"Have you met someone?" I asked her.

"No." Ma frowned at me as if I'd asked something rude, then pulled a baking sheet with fish patties out of the oven. She placed two on each of our plates and poured the red mass next to them — canned spaghetti with fish patties. Seriously.

I put two glasses of water on the table, and we sat down. "We can put your tips in the savings account for our down payment," I said.

"We might need the money for a new car," Ma said. "The Volvo is losing oil."

"Have you had it checked?"

"Karl at the garage said it's beyond repair," she replied. "He looked at it without charge."

"I wish Dad were here to repair it. I'd hate to lose his Volvo," I muttered, staring down at my plate. I really didn't like eating the tomato sauce with the fish. Together the two tasted like metal.

Ma picked up her glass and took a sip. I could hear her swallow.

"You know that I don't want to talk about your dad," she said. She gave me a warning look before she got up, rinsed her plate in the sink, and slammed the plate down on the counter.

"Nothing happens when you say it," I whispered. "Dad, Dad, Dad."

But it was too late. Ma had already disappeared into her bedroom. I was left at the table, feeling sick to my stomach. I scraped the rest of my dinner into the garbage and drank more water to get the taste out of my mouth.

I looked out the window, feeling the cloud pressing down on me with its familiar loneliness and pain. I didn't even want to go out to bury roadkill. I wanted to talk to someone who cared. I needed to apologize to Theo.

18

I rehearsed what I was going to say to Theo on my way to school the next day, but when I arrived, he wasn't there. Sitting next to his empty chair made me feel even worse, and I wished I could go to his house right after school. But it was Thursday, and I was supposed to go with Carrie to the animal shelter.

We had arranged to meet at the shelter at four-thirty. I was on time, but Carrie looked annoyed when she got there five minutes late.

"Everything okay?" I asked.

She just shrugged and mumbled, "Yeah," and I remembered that she'd really wanted to come here with Victoria.

When we rang the shelter's bell, a lanky young woman with a nose ring opened the gate. Her T-shirt had the words *LOVE A DOG — ADOPT* printed in black letters around the outline of a dog's head. I liked her immediately, but Carrie got that arrogant look on her face that she used on people she found unattractive.

"Hey," the woman said. "I'm Spring. Which one of you is Wren?"

"That's me," I said.

"What an awesome name," Spring said. "I should have named myself after a bird."

"My dad called you and —" Carrie said.

"I know," Spring interrupted. "You're here to walk Kimbra and Kyle." She motioned for us to follow her, and we trailed along as she strode toward a flat-roofed building.

"What kind of a hippie is she?" Carrie asked in a snotty whisper. I didn't answer.

We passed through a narrow corridor with metal cages on both sides. Dogs of different sizes and colors greeted us with frantic barks. I stopped to take a closer look at a puppy that hadn't joined the crazy chorus.

"Why does he look so sad?" I asked.

"His mother died recently, and all his siblings have been adopted," Spring replied.

"Why didn't anyone take him?"

"Beats me," Spring said with a shrug. "Maybe because he's just not as pretty as his siblings."

"I think he's cute," I said, sticking my hand through the bars to pet him. "You should adopt him, Carrie."

"Are you looking for a dog?" Spring asked. "Your dad just said you wanted to volunteer to get some experience with dogs."

"I'm looking for a dog, but I want a pedigree dog, not some mutt," Carrie said with a huff.

"You should take one of ours," Spring said. "They'll love you forever."

"I don't like him," Carrie said, crossing her arms. "Look how his one ear is smaller than the other."

"You know what they say — beauty is in the eye of the beholder," Spring said.

I was embarrassed for Carrie and could tell that Spring found her annoying. "Where are these two dogs you want us to walk?" I asked.

"Right here," Spring said, leading us to a cage at the end of the corridor. "Meet Kimbra and Kyle."

A heavy black Labrador mix and a short-legged brownish dog with a pug nose squeezed their muzzles through the cage door.

"They look funny," I said.

"I can't believe my dad made me do this," Carrie muttered. "They're so ugly."

"I don't think they're ugly," I said. "I think they're kind of cute."

"Look, the big one has a scar on his forehead. It's gross," Carrie said.

"What's so bad about a scar? Maybe someone abused the poor doggie," I said. "Look how happy it makes them that we're here."

We took the dogs outside, but as we walked, my mind wandered back to Ma's new hairdo. I had to get it off my chest. "I'm worried that my mother is seeing someone."

"What makes you think that?" Carrie asked.

"She got her hair done," I said.

Carrie shook her head. "My mother does that every week. What's the problem?"

"Just what I said — she might have met a new man," I said. "In the past two months, whenever my mom has started dating a guy, it's only lasted a few weeks. Then they break up, and we have to move."

"That's too bad," Carrie said. But I could tell that she didn't really care. She quickly changed the subject. "My mom asked me what I wanted to do for my birthday party."

"When's your birthday?" I asked.

"In two weeks," Carrie said.

"You know," I started to say, "I would really like to stay here in Pyramid, but I'm worried —"

"I want her to take all the girls to her beauty salon," Carrie interrupted as if I hadn't spoken. "Hair, nails, makeup . . . I think that would be fun."

I didn't say anything. Carrie clearly didn't want to listen.

Just then, Kyle stopped to lift his leg, and Kimbra found a place to do her big business.

"Do I have to pick this up?" Carrie asked, her face scrunched up.

"I guess that's why Spring gave us these bags," I said, pulling one out of my pocket. "I'll hold her leash for you."

With obvious disgust, Carrie bent down to scoop up the poop and hurried to drop the bag in a trash can. We continued walking, and Carrie continued talking about her birthday party.

"When we go to the salon, you can get highlights," she said. "Like your mom."

"I just told you, I don't like her highlights," I said. "I'm worried she's wasting money to look good for a new guy she just met."

"You wouldn't have to pay for yours," Carrie said. "You'd get a free haircut, too."

I was hurt but tried not to show it. "Let's head back to the shelter and drop off the dogs," I suggested.

"Good idea," Carrie agreed. "I'm over this."

As we walked back, Carrie continued to talk about her birthday party. She didn't even seem to notice that I didn't respond.

19

I was in no hurry to get to school the next morning. I didn't really want to share my homework with Carrie, but I knew she would expect it. Sure enough, she saw me entering the main hall and waved at me. I pretended not to see her and walked quickly toward the stairs. Maybe she should get her homework from somebody else today.

No such luck — Carrie followed me. "Did you do the math word problems?" she asked.

I stopped. "Yes."

"Could I get them from you?"

I should have said no, but I didn't. Instead, I nodded and took out my notebook. She took it and squatted down on the stairs to write down my answers.

"Can you believe my dad?" Carrie asked as she turned the page of her notebook. "Now he's making me help out at the landfill office on Saturday to file papers." She looked up at me, and I could tell she was waiting for some reaction.

"That's too bad," I said.

"This is all about my birthday," Carrie continued. "He wants to show my mom and me that he's in charge. My mom thinks it's crazy too. She wants me to have a dog." She handed me back my notebook. "Thank you. You're the best."

I started to reply, but Carrie was already headed down the hallway. She stopped suddenly and turned around. "Oh, we have to go to the shelter again on Tuesday," she called before she quickened her steps to catch up with Victoria.

I knew Carrie didn't want to go back to the shelter. And, of course, she didn't even ask if I had time to go with her again. Or if I even wanted to.

* * *

In the afternoon, we had gym. I usually looked forward to it, even though the girls' changing room smelled like old socks and chewing gum. I quickly changed into my shorts and T-shirt and headed back to the gym.

A few minutes later Theo came out of the changing room, wearing these hideous sports glasses tied around his head with a thick black elastic band. Callum nudged Tim and said, "Uhh, the four-eyed monster is coming. Beware!"

It only got worse when we learned that our P.E. teacher was out sick, and a substitute teacher would be instructing the class instead. While the substitute took attendance, Callum crawled behind Theo and hissed in his ear, "Hey, cross-eyed monster. Which planet are you from?"

When Theo didn't respond, Callum pinched him until Theo turned around, staring at Callum through his outlandish goggles. I could tell the teasing was starting to get to him. There were some giggles, and then Carrie said, loud enough for everyone to hear, "Theo looks like a freakish monster."

"A shortsighted one," Victoria added, making everyone laugh.

I got angry. I had seen the other kids tease him before, but today it bothered me as much as if it was happening to me instead of him. They should have left him alone. It wasn't Theo's fault that he had to wear those glasses. The others didn't know anything about his mother or the way his father had changed since her death.

The substitute teacher looked up from the class list and asked us to be quiet. After just a few gymnastic exercises, he let us play dodgeball. Callum and Victoria picked the teams. I usually got chosen for a team right at the beginning since I can run fast and turn quickly. Plus I throw a mean, strong ball — another important skill for dodgeball.

Callum picked me right after he called Tom to join his team. Victoria picked Carrie to join her team, even though she was clumsy. Theo was the last kid standing, and since it was Callum's turn to choose, Theo ended up with us.

The teams spread out, each on their own side of the gym. With ten kids on each team and four balls in play, people were eliminated quickly. Callum aimed at Victoria, and she screamed when the ball hit her foot.

"Victoria is out!" Callum called, smiling gleefully. He tried to dodge a ball coming at him from the right, but it was too late. The ball smacked him on the shoulder, bounced once, and Theo caught it. Callum looked surprised, but he had to leave the field.

Soon, Theo and I were the only kids left standing on our team. Carrie stood on the opposite side, staring at us.

"Aim at Carrie's legs," I whispered in Theo's ear. "She's a bad catcher and can't bend down quickly."

Theo hurled the ball at Carrie. She tried to move out of the way, but the ball glanced off her knee.

"Oh no! I'm out!" Carrie cried before she walked off.

Later, in the changing room, she confronted me. "How come you helped Theo like that?"

"How come you can't stop talking about his appearance?" I asked.

"Oh, so you're defending your boyfriend now?" she asked.

I could hear Victoria giggle.

"He's not my boyfriend, and you know it," I said. "I just wish you guys would stop being mean to him."

* * *

After school, I waited for Theo at the bike rack. "Hey," I said when he walked up. "How are you?"

"Okay," he replied, not looking at me. "Thanks for helping me in dodgeball."

"I'm sorry, Theo, about what I said the other day at the pond. I didn't mean to say that. I feel bad about it, and I want to apologize."

Theo looked down at the space between his feet, leaving a long pause, and I prepared myself for being turned down. I'd deserve it, too.

Please, say something.

"So you realize that it's not *your* pond and those aren't *your* birds?" he finally asked.

"I do," I said, nodding. "And if you still want to, I'd like to watch birds together. I was even wondering if . . . maybe we could add your photos to our report. It would make it more powerful."

Another pause. Theo adjusted his backpack. "Good idea," he said. "We'll add them to our poster so people can see what they'll be losing if the landfill gets expanded. But the report is due the day after tomorrow. We don't have a lot of time."

"Let's meet tomorrow morning," I suggested. "Mornings are better to watch birds anyway."

"What time?" he asked.

"Around six-thirty," I said.

Theo nodded. "I'll be there."

20

The next morning the sky was clear and the air was still. The pond sparkled in the bright morning sun. When I arrived, Theo was waiting.

"I note all my bird sightings in my notebook," I said. When we reached the boulder, I took out my bird journal. "You write down time and place, describe the bird, and then make a drawing." I showed him a few sample pages. "My drawings are bad."

"This one's good." He pointed to a great blue heron that Dad had drawn for me.

"My dad did that one."

"He's a good drawer."

"Mm-hmm," I said, hoping he didn't take it any further.

"Is your dad a bird-watcher too?"

I was quiet for a moment. "He was. He's dead."

Now he knew. It was out there, and there was no taking it back.

"When did he die?" Theo asked.

"Last February," I replied. *Please don't ask how he died.*

Thankfully all Theo said was, "That's not a very long time ago."

Suddenly, the crow, Joseph, was back and drawing attention to himself. *Caw, caw, caw!*

Theo got out his camera. "He's looking at us," he said.

"I know," I replied.

Just then Theo noticed the drawing I'd done of Joseph. "That's not a bad drawing of that crow," he said. "Good job with its head." He pointed to the page and the word written there. "You gave the bird a name?"

"I did," I said, waiting for a snide comment.

"Was your dad's name Joseph?" he asked.

"No," I said. *Please, don't ask any more questions about Dad.*

"Did you know that in India people believe you can get reborn as an animal?" Theo asked, seemingly out of the blue.

"Hmm," I said, keeping my eyes on my journal.

"After my mom died, my dad bought all these books about grieving," he continued. "I tried to read them, and he wanted to talk about them with me. But I didn't understand all of it. I used to wonder what kind of animal my mother would come back as. In church, they tell you dead people are angels, but I'd rather think of her as a bird or butterfly."

I knew Theo probably only wanted to give me an opportunity to talk about Dad, but I didn't want to hear about death anymore. "Let's walk around the pond," I suggested, taking off.

Walking felt good, pushing the cloud away from me, leaving enough room to breathe. I relaxed.

"I don't know if I believe people come back as animals," I said after several minutes. "I miss my dad the way he was."

"I know," Theo said. "I got kind of angry at my dad for talking about this stuff. I even yelled at him that it was all garbage, made up by people who don't know how much it hurts."

"Have you heard of those stages of grieving?" I asked.

Theo nodded. "I have. But I don't believe in them. I never denied that my mother died. And I wasn't angry either. I can't remember the other stages, but I think counselors just make this stuff up."

The cloud lifted further, and I took a deep breath. We kept walking. It was good to be silent with Theo.

Along the way, we heard a familiar caw.

"Look, there's Joseph," Theo said, pointing ahead to where the crow stood in front of what looked like an animal's burrow under a tree. He was picking at something.

"He must have found some dead animal," I said, focusing my binoculars on it.

Theo turned his camera toward Joseph and zoomed in. "It looks like he's trying to get a turtle out of its shell."

Joseph kept pecking at the turtle for a while before he gave up and flew away. I walked over to pick it up.

"It's just a shell," I said. "No turtle in it anymore."

"But the shell is complete. Look at these holes, though," I said, pointing to two small round holes on the top and two on the bottom that perforated the shell.

"I think this is a box turtle shell. I have a book about turtles at home. But the holes don't look like they were made by Joseph's beak," Theo said.

"I'll keep it," I said, picking the shell up and sticking it in my backpack. As we walked away, we saw a killdeer limping.

"Oh no," Theo said. "It must be injured."

I shook my head. "That's called the broken-wing impression. She pretends to be injured so a possible predator will come after her instead of her nest. We must've come close to her nest, and she's trying to protect her eggs."

"It's cool that you know all this stuff about birds," Theo said.

I looked away. It felt too weird to hear a compliment from him.

"It's time for us to go," I said.

We headed back to our bikes in silence, but as we pedaled toward the school, I glanced over at him. I was really glad that Theo wanted to watch birds with me.

21

The next morning Ma told me she would be home late that night, and I shouldn't wait up for her.

"Where are you going? I asked.

"Oh, it's my coworker's birthday. We reserved a table at the diner."

"Whose birthday is it?" I asked suspiciously.

"You don't know her," Ma said.

"What's her name?"

"Her name is Tricia," she said, frowning. "Why are you interrogating me?"

"I'm not. I'm just asking," I said.

When she got ready to leave for work, Ma checked her hair in the mirror, and I looked for more suspicious signs.

But she wore her usual work clothes and didn't put on any makeup. Maybe there was nothing to worry about after all.

* * *

After school Theo and I met at the library to work on our report. I was surprised to find myself looking forward to it. But the truth was, I liked Theo. I liked spending time with him, and it felt good to share the bird-watching with someone.

Mrs. Russo came over to greet us and looked through Theo's photos. "These are wonderful," she said.

"It's really a great place," Theo said. "Too bad they're turning it into a Dumpster."

"It is a shame," Mrs. Russo agreed, holding a photo of a female chickadee.

"I wish we could do more than just write a school report. I wish we could actually *do* something about it," I said.

Mrs. Russo looked up and said, "We could display the photos in the library showcase. At least the readers of Pyramid will see them and learn that Pete's Pond is about to be destroyed. What do you think, Theo? Would you allow me to display your photos? I would put your names in there as well."

Theo nodded. "We could make posters and label the birds and explain that their home is in danger," he said.

Mrs. Russo turned to me. "Are you okay with that, Wren? We usually just keep flyers and announcements about local events in the showcase. This would give it a much better use."

"I think that's a great idea," I said.

"All right then," Mrs. Russo said. "I'll let you get on with your work. Good luck with the report. Come back as soon as you can to put the display in the case."

We sat down by the window at the back of the library and began to sort through the slides for our presentation. Outside in the parking lot, I saw a man and a woman walking toward a car. He opened the door for her, and before she got in, they quickly kissed. Watching them reminded me of my conversation with Ma this morning and that worried feeling grew again in my stomach.

"Are you okay?" Theo asked.

"I'm fine," I said, pointing to the screen. "This great blue heron should go on the other side of the text."

"You don't seem fine. You're brooding."

"I am not." I knew Theo was right — I was brooding — but I didn't want to admit it.

"All right," Theo said. "If you say so."

"I'm worried my mother has a new boyfriend!" I blurted out. There! I'd said it!

Theo answered with one of his famous pauses. Then he asked, "How do you know that?"

"She has a new fancy hairdo," I said.

"That's good evidence, but it's not conclusive," Theo said. "Did you ask her about it?"

"Yes," I said. "She said she's not, but I don't believe her. Before we moved here we lived in two places, and each time, after about two weeks, she started dating someone. We've lived here for almost three weeks now."

"Would it be that bad if she really did meet a man?" Theo asked.

"It'd be very bad. You have no idea! They break up, she cries, and then we have to move. It's happened the same way in the past two towns."

"It could be different this time," he said.

I shook my head. "I don't think so."

Theo was quiet for a while as we continued to check the slides. Then he said, "I wish I could say that about my dad."

"Say what?" I asked.

"That he's in love. Or that he's met someone. That would be a good thing."

"I don't understand."

"You're upset because you think you'll lose something if your mother falls in love. I understand it hasn't been that long since your dad died . . . but at least she's trying. My dad has totally given up. He hasn't even looked at another woman since my mother died." Then he added in a low voice, "Actually, he's stopped everything."

I didn't say anything. I felt sheepish after having shared my own concerns about Ma dating too much.

With his pencil, Theo drew a line along the margin of his notebook. "He spends all his time with books." He pressed a little harder on his pencil, and the line on the paper became darker. "I wish he'd meet a woman who would cheer him up."

"I'm sorry," I said. That's all I could say.

Theo shrugged. "You don't need to be sorry. It's just a different way of looking at things."

He turned the pencil around and began to erase the line he'd just drawn. The paper creased from the impact of his rubbing, leaving the line imprinted on the page.

22

I stopped at the pond before school the next day, hoping that sitting on the boulder might help clear my head. I didn't really want to get to school early to deliver my homework to Carrie. She was selfish and only wanted to talk about herself. I got hurt spending time with her. Why did I continue trying to fit in with her? Did I really need to pretend to be like her if it only made me miserable?

I knew I shouldn't let Carrie copy my homework anymore. But I worried that if I stopped helping her, she and Victoria would make my life miserable. It would take a lot of courage to say no to her, and I didn't know if I could do it.

White and gray clouds dashed across the sky, and I could smell rain in the distance. I wondered if I would get wet soon. If Dad had been here, he would have sung me the song from *Winnie the Pooh and the Blustery Day*.

I didn't want to think about it, but the song reminded me of how Dad and I had made fun of the words *thrustily* and *gustily*. We would crack up trying to outdo each other using them in sentences.

"I am *thrustily* throwing the garbage in the trash can," I'd say.

And he would respond, "Your comment makes me laugh quite *gustily*."

I tried to focus on the blue jay in the tree on my left while the song kept playing in my head. Suddenly, the sky started to spit icy pellets. I put away my journal and binoculars, ran back to my bike, and pedaled to school as fast as I could, squinting against the wind. While the hail whipped my face, I suddenly remembered a quote from another Winnie the Pooh movie that Dad had liked:

"If ever there is tomorrow when we're not together . . . there is something you must always remember. You are braver than you believe, stronger than you seem, and smarter than you think. But the most important thing is, even if we're apart . . . I'll always be with you."

* * *

Later that morning, Theo and I presented our report. Mrs. Peters gave us an *A*-. The few deductions were due to Theo's lack of eye contact with the audience, but I didn't mind the slightly lower grade. Looking directly at people while talking was just not his thing.

After class, Carrie caught up with me. "Why did you say all that bad stuff about my dad? In your report, you made him out to be some criminal."

"Our report wasn't about your dad. We argued that the township should protect Pete's Pond," I said. "We were supposed to talk about a controversial issue, and we did."

"I just can't believe you're making such a big deal out of it," Carrie said. "My dad is just doing his job."

"He's destroying a beautiful piece of nature," I said. "And I wish he wouldn't."

"You want to tell him how to run his business?" she asked, glaring at me.

Theo suddenly appeared next to us. "We were just trying to raise some awareness," he said.

"Awareness?" Carrie repeated, making the word sound like a disease.

"Yes, awareness," he said. "The ability to feel or be aware of events around one's self. You should try it sometime."

Carrie's mouth dropped open — I wasn't sure if it was shock or outrage that had silenced her. Finally she straightened up and said, "The two of you are just two crazy peas in a pod." Then she stomped off.

"Thanks," I said to Theo once Carrie was gone.

"You're welcome," he answered. We started walking down the hall together. "I'd like to ask you something."

"Go ahead."

"I talked to my dad about a new pair of glasses, and we're getting them soon. I also told him I needed some new clothes. We haven't shopped for clothes since my mother died. He doesn't want to go to the mall and said we should order them from a catalog. I think that's a bad idea. I wanted to ask you . . ." He hesitated. "Would you ask your mother to take me to the mall to buy new clothes?

I mean, it would obviously be you and me and your mom going to the mall. Together. I don't know. It's probably a bad idea." He looked down, avoiding eye contact.

For a moment I hesitated to commit. What if Carrie or Victoria saw us at the store? But then I realized it didn't really matter. I didn't care if they saw us or not.

"Yeah, no problem," I said. "I can ask my mother. She's off on Saturday, and I'm sure she'd take us. Let's do it then."

23

"How did you do?" Mrs. Russo asked when we visited her at the library the next afternoon. We had dropped off the photos and poster the day before, and Mrs. Russo had asked us to check back in with her. "Your exhibition is quite popular. Many patrons have commented on it."

"Too bad it won't make any difference," I muttered. "The township will vote in ten days and just give Mr. Zusack the land."

"That's a gloomy outlook, Wren," Mrs. Russo said. "You shouldn't be so pessimistic. At least more people are informed about what's going on. Who knows, something might come out of it."

"I hope you're right," I said. "But I still wish we could do more."

"We should write to a state senator," Theo suggested.

I shook my head. "We'll just get one of those canned letters that says, 'Thank you for expressing your concern ... blah, blah, blah ...'"

"But look at the headline in the paper," Theo said, picking up the copy of the *Soo Enquirer* on the circulation desk. "Senator Larsson is coming to the Soo the Saturday after next. That could be our chance."

"He's not going to talk to us," I said, taking the newspaper and skimming the article.

"You could at least try," Mrs. Russo said.

"What if we wrote a petition and collected signatures?" Theo suggested. "Remember when we talked about civil actions in social studies class? We read that article about people in Detroit who submitted a petition signed by a thousand people to save an old train station from demolition?"

"We won't find a thousand people in Pyramid," I said.

"You won't need a thousand," Mrs. Russo said. "Even if you only collect fifty signatures and submit them to the township board with a petition, they'd see that it's not just two kids who want to preserve Pete's Pond. Many adults think that way too."

"I could ask my dad to take it to the university," Theo said, sounding enthused.

"And I'll point out the petition to patrons at the circulation desk," Mrs. Russo said.

I had to agree. It did sound like a good idea.

"I could take it to Mr. Leroy's store," I offered. "And we could collect signatures at the farmer's market on that Saturday when the senator is here." I held up the newspaper. "It says that the TV station will be there to film him talking to people. We could bring along a poster or something to hold up when we're with him. If we do something out of the usual, we might get on TV too."

"Now you're getting the right attitude," Mrs. Russo said, giving me a thumbs-up.

"Where can we find out about petitions?" Theo asked.

"Let me see." Mrs. Russo turned in her chair and typed on her computer keyboard. "I think I can help you draft the text."

* * *

"You said you needed shirts and pants," Ma said as we entered JCPenney on Saturday morning.

When I'd told her about Theo's request, I'd waited for some comment from her regarding him being a boy and such. But she hadn't said anything, just asked when we wanted to go.

"Yes," Theo said, as we walked past the men's section toward the back of the store.

"Let's start with pants," Ma said, stopping in front of a shelf with jeans. "Do you want slim fit or flexible waist?"

Theo looked at me and shrugged. "Slim fit," I said.

"What size are you?"

"I think a twenty-four," Theo said.

"Here, these might be good." Ma pulled a pair off the shelf and held them out in front of him. "We'll bring you another size if this one doesn't fit."

Theo disappeared into the fitting room, and Ma and I looked for shirts.

"Do you think he'd like this?" she asked, holding up a long sleeved T-shirt with a picture of a truck printed on the front.

"No," I said, shaking my head. "He's a basics only kind of guy. Nothing too funky."

"How about this one?" Ma asked, pointing to a dark-green long-sleeve T-shirt.

"That's better," I said.

"It's kind of fun to shop for a boy," Ma commented.

Doesn't it remind you of shopping for Dad? I wanted to ask. But I knew that kind of comment would darken her good mood. She certainly wouldn't start talking about Dad while we were at JCPenney with Theo. So I let it go.

Just this one time, I told myself.

"What do you guys think?" Theo asked just then. He had come out of the changing room and was looking at himself in the mirror. The jeans fit well.

"Perfect," Ma and I said in unison.

24

On Wednesday afternoon it was my turn to clean the apartment. I was straightening up Ma's room when I noticed a small plastic bag on her dresser. As I moved it aside to dust, I couldn't help but peek inside — a lacy black bra and matching underpants stared out at me. The label said they were made of silk. The price tags were still on both the items — thirty dollars each.

Why did Ma need expensive silk underwear? She'd always told me that underwear had to be made from practical cotton to tolerate hot temperatures when washed.

A cold, anxious feeling rose inside me like dark water. This was a clear sign. Ma had found another Mr. Someone.

What was I going to do? I hadn't been able to prevent it from happening the past two times.

For a brief moment I wished Dad were here so I could talk to him about it. Now *that* was crazy. Obviously, I couldn't talk to my dad about the other men Ma was dating. But he'd always had this way of making my worries go away.

"Let them flutter," he'd tell me, waving a hand in the air. If he saw me frowning, he'd say, "You're still holding on to it." Then he would reach over and tickle my stomach, adding, "Laughing always helps."

And it had.

But now I couldn't find my sense of humor. And I couldn't make the worries flutter away. Instead, the dark water kept rising, and by the time I finished the dishes, something in me had snapped.

I searched the apartment. I looked in Ma's drawers, in her closet, in the bathroom vanity. I didn't even know exactly *what* I was looking for. But at the same time, I was terrified of what I might find.

In the living room I spotted several of Ma's romance novels scattered on the side table next to the sofa. That was her new obsession. For as long as I could remember she'd read detective stories, but now she only brought home books with a guy in an open shirt on the cover. They all had titles like *Loved Again*, *The Wolf at the Door*, and *Exposure*.

I headed back into Ma's bedroom. On her nightstand, she'd left her planner. I wanted to look inside, but I knew it would be wrong to snoop. But then I thought about the bra and my suspicions. That settled it. I opened the planner.

The form for the post office with our forwarding address was still tucked in a pocket inside the front cover. So she still hadn't sent it.

I slowly turned to this week's entries. The words *Greg, Chez Amide Café, 4 p.m.* were scribbled on tomorrow's date. Greg? Who was Greg?

Just then I heard a key rattle in the door and quickly put the planner back where I'd found it. I raced back to the living room and sat down on the sofa with my back to the door, pretending to look for something in my backpack.

Ma came in and headed straight for the kitchen. "Chinese or Mexican — which one do you want?" she called.

"I'll take Mexican."

"I can't eat with you," she added. "I'm already late for work. But I needed to grab this."

It was safe to turn now, and when I did, I saw Ma holding the plastic bag from her nightstand. She pulled the silk bra out and let it dangle from her index finger.

"Can you believe it?" she asked. "My coworker Deborah gave me this set of underwear. It doesn't fit her, and the store won't take it back since she doesn't have the receipt anymore. She left it in my locker with a note." Ma shook her head. "As if I would wear a silk bra. I'll give it back to her tonight."

* * *

After Ma had left, I breathed a sigh of relief. The bra had turned out to be nothing to worry about. But there was still the entry with a man's name in her planner. I could have asked Ma about Greg, but I was too afraid to hear that he was the new Mr. Someone.

Instead, I decided to go on a mission to obtain information by visual observation — or according to Mr. Leroy, *reconnaissance.*

25

The best spot to overlook the entrance to Chez Amide turned out to be inside the Northern Lights Bookshop across the street. After school, I positioned myself next to the paperback shelf by the window and waited.

Ma was almost on time. I could tell she'd come directly from work. She wore the same shirt and cardigan combination she'd put on that morning. In front of the café, she stopped to take out her little mirror and freshen up her lipstick. But she didn't enter the coffee shop; instead she just waited outside.

A few minutes later, a white Volvo station wagon, a newer model than ours, slowly drove by. The driver waved to Ma as he passed, then parked a bit farther up the street.

He got out, and she walked toward him. They shook hands. No kiss — not yet.

Greg looked older than the other guys Ma had dated. He was even a bit shorter than Ma and wore a tweed cap. A tweed cap! After a moment, they walked toward the parked car and stood next to it for a while, talking, smiling, and admiring the vehicle.

I wondered if she was telling him that her dead husband had driven a similar car. Would she say dead or deceased? Or did she call Dad her *late* husband? I'd overheard her saying that to the landlady once. Who'd made up that expression? It wasn't fooling anyone. A dead person is not late. A dead person is dead. A dead person won't be coming back later.

Mr. Tweed Cap threw the keys over to Ma. She caught them, all smiles, and got in on the driver's side. Greg stepped in on the passenger side, and they drove off.

* * *

When I got home, the white Volvo stood in the driveway. I raced upstairs and slammed the door to our apartment behind me.

"Where is he?" I demanded.

"Who?" Ma asked from the sofa, putting her romance novel down.

"The man who drives the Volvo?"

"Which man?" she asked.

"I saw you earlier at Chez Amide with a guy wearing a tweed cap. His car is in the driveway."

"He's not here," Ma said, frowning. "I bought the Volvo from him."

"What? What about Dad's car?"

"I told you it was beyond repair."

"How much did you take from the savings account?" I demanded.

"Eight hundred dollars," Ma said, sounding irritated. "Are you going to make a big deal out of this?"

"It *is* a big deal," I said. "It's my money, too."

"I needed wheels, and this was the cheapest way to get them."

"You should have told me," I insisted.

"I told you that Karl said the old Volvo couldn't be fixed."

"Dad loved that car," I said. "He called it Sven, his trusted Swedish workhorse."

Ma got up and walked toward me. "It had to be done," she said quietly. "There's no point in keeping a broken car."

She took another step in my direction, but I backed away. "How could you do that? It was the last thing we had of Dad's!" With the back of my hand I wiped away a tear.

"Come here, Wren," Ma said.

But I didn't want her to touch me. I could hardly breathe. I had to get away from her. In that moment, I was so mad I almost hated her.

* * *

For a while I pedaled around aimlessly, looking for roadkill. Placing a dead animal in the ground would have made me feel calmer — maybe. I wasn't even sure of that anymore. But I couldn't find one and decided to go to the pond, hoping Theo would be there.

I knew it was unlikely — he'd told me in school that he had to go to the dentist — but I still imagined him waiting on the boulder. He would have listened, and I would have felt better just by telling him.

But when I reached the pond, our usual spot was empty.

I picked up a pebble and threw it into the pond, watching the rings widen and ripple across the water. The cloud was pressing down on me once again. I couldn't tell if the extra pain came more from missing Dad, or from the way Ma had hurt me.

A bird's nasal yammering echoed through the forest. I knew which bird made that sound and looked for the white-breasted nuthatch in the trees. Then a small hawk, a kind I didn't recognize, appeared. It had a blue-gray upper body and rufous bars on white underneath. Dark red eyes. Wings short and rounded. Tail long, squared with heavy bars. Yellow legs and feet.

I had brought my backpack with my bird book and journal with me, and I pulled them both out. My bird book said it was a sharp-shinned hawk. I wrote its name in my journal. Next to it, I wrote the date, location, and weather. Then I tried to draw the bird, but it flew away too quickly.

If Theo were here, he could have taken a photo. I shook my head to clear it. Why did I keep thinking of Theo?

On my way home, I found a raccoon lying dead on the road. Its head was smashed, and part of its brain had leaked out on the asphalt. I got off my bike, put on my gloves, and dug a shallow hole near the shoulder. The raccoon was too big for the trowel, and I had to pick it up with my hands. I dropped it into the hole and pushed the soil over it.

When I was finished, I jumped on my bike. I pedaled hard and fast, waiting for the relief I usually felt when the burning in my lungs singed away the pain of missing Dad. But it didn't work. The cloud had turned purple.

26

The next morning our first period was English. Ma and I had not spoken since I learned about the Volvo. She'd already left for the diner by the time I got home and had worked late, then slept in this morning. That was probably for the best since I was still so mad at her.

At school I couldn't focus on the novel we were reading in class. The book was about a kid — an orphan — called Maniac Magee who could run fast. I could relate. I felt like I'd lost both parents too.

In Spanish class we discussed holidays and family traditions. Mrs. Quezada wanted us to come up with a new holiday — an invented one that could become a new tradition in our families, like a half birthday or a monthly picnic. We were supposed to make a poster with a description of the new holiday and a drawing to illustrate what we would do on the day. The idea was that we would show our posters to our parents during the portfolio night at the end of the week. I knew Ma would attend.

Everyone was really excited. All around the room, kids were calling out their ideas. Callum wanted to celebrate his dog's birthday, and Victoria dreamed up a Pink Day when she and her mother would only wear her favorite color.

Mrs. Quezada had a hard time reminding everyone that this was a Spanish assignment. *"En Español, por favor,"* she pleaded.

I made a poster with a drawing of an airplane flying over the ocean. Then I printed *Dia del Padre Muerto* in big black letters in the sky. At the bottom, I drew the two of us — Ma and me — on the beach. Tiny little stick figures, dressed in black.

Mrs. Quezada had said that during portfolio night, our parents would be invited to talk to us about the new holiday. Ma would have to look at it with me. This time she could not run away. I would have created an irreversible situation. One that couldn't be altered by those affected.

A *fait accompli.*

* * *

At lunch, I met Carrie in line in the cafeteria. There was a plate with two lettuce leaves, three slices of tomato, and a carrot stick on her tray. I picked up two slices of pizza, and she frowned at me. "Aren't you worried that you'll get fat eating all that greasy food?"

"No, I'm not worried. I like pizza," I said, taking a big bite.

There were two seats available at the table near the door, and Carrie and I sat down opposite each other. Her eyes searched the cafeteria, but our teacher had asked Victoria to stay back and finish an art assignment.

At the other end of the cafeteria, I saw Theo sit down. Why hadn't I waited to have lunch with him? I certainly didn't want to share what was on my mind with Carrie.

We ate in silence for a while. Carrie scooped up a lettuce leaf with her fork and balanced it carefully. Then she suddenly blurted out, "I heard you're exhibiting your bird photos at the library and collecting signatures for a petition against my dad's landfill."

"We're just collecting signatures," I said. "It's not a big deal." I was thinking about Ma and didn't have any patience for Carrie's hysterics.

"I can't believe you're doing this to me," she said. "Making my dad out to be some evil destroyer of nature."

"I'm not doing anything to you." I looked at her and added, "Not everything is about you."

Carrie inhaled sharply and glared at me. "You probably just want to hurt my dad because you don't have one."

Suddenly the kids at the tables nearby grew quiet. Everyone was watching.

I didn't know how Carrie had found out about my dad. I was mad at her for saying that, and at the same time, I was scared of what I felt the need to do next.

Then I heard Dad's words again: *You are braver than you think you are.*

I slowly got up, not saying a word. But before I left, I paused and looked down at Carrie. My voice was calm when I said, "I don't think I want to have anything to do with you anymore."

27

I waited for the terrible remorse to wash over me. But it didn't come. Instead, I felt relieved. It was time. I had to get away from Carrie. It was a good thing that I'd walked out on her.

But my relief only lasted so long. My mood was as blustery as the weather. I was supposed to work at Mr. Leroy's store that afternoon, but by the time I reached Eats of Eden, there were still too many feelings churning inside of me. I was worried that I had crossed the invisible line. I had stepped away from popular girls to the other side, where lonely nerds like Theo had to hang out. From now on, Theo and I would spend more time together — even at recess — and work together on all class projects.

What would I do when the others started whispering about Theo and me? Would I be able to stand it?

Mr. Leroy noticed that something was bothering me, so I told him what had happened.

"If this girl is mean and you have nothing in common with her, you did the right thing," Mr. Leroy advised as we unpacked a box of gluten-free crackers in the back of the store. "Why worry about spending more time with Theo? I thought you got along well with that boy."

That was the problem with adults. They always made everything sound so easy.

"I do get along with him," I said. "But what if —"

"Now don't tell me you can't be friends because he's a boy," Mr. Leroy interrupted. I had mentioned during a previous shift that I was working with Theo on the social studies project and that we had started to watch birds together. "From all I hear, you have a lot in common with him and you enjoy spending time together. That's the most important thing. What do you *not* like about him?"

"It's not that I don't *like* him," I said.

"You see?" Mr. Leroy said. "You can't come up with anything. So I say, just hang out with Theo, and things will be all right."

* * *

Theo was waiting for me at the bike racks before school the next day. "I heard what happened in the cafeteria yesterday," he said.

I locked up my bicycle, and we walked up the stairs together. Callum and a bunch of other boys were standing in the corner, right next to the office. When he saw us walking by, he called out to the other boys, "Look, it's the newlyweds!"

Everyone laughed.

I looked straight ahead and headed toward my locker. I put my backpack away and followed Theo to the other end of the hallway where a row of desks waited to be fixed by the janitor.

"You can't let it get to you," Theo said, pushing himself onto one of them.

"Mm-hmm." I nodded.

"Seriously," he said. "They can only hurt you if you let it bother you."

"This doesn't bother you?" I asked.

Theo shook his head. "Not anymore," he said. "I play this little game with myself. Whenever someone says something mean, I count to three and think of that person naked in front of Mrs. Peters's class. Imagine Callum, with his fat little legs, standing naked in front of us. That makes me laugh."

I had to smile.

"Don't be scared," Theo told me. "You cut yourself loose from Carrie. That's a good thing."

Right now it didn't feel too good. In the distance, I could see Carrie and Victoria talking, throwing glances in our direction.

"You're not like them," Theo continued. "Now you don't have to pretend anymore. And trust me, if you don't respond to their teasing, they'll get bored and leave you alone."

Just then, the bell rang, and we walked back toward the classroom. On the way, I saw something now hanging on my locker door. Someone had cut a heart out of pink construction paper. On it were two letters: *T & W*.

"Pay no attention to it," Theo whispered.

Mrs. Peters greeted us at the door. "Good morning! I changed the seating arrangement. I'm sure you'll all be glad to learn that you are now free to choose who you want to sit with."

Sure enough, the desks were now arranged in sets of two. Carrie and Victoria had already grabbed seats next to each other. Callum and Tim raced to another pair of desks.

Theo hesitated for a moment, looking at me. Carrie nudged Victoria in the side so she'd watch what I'd do.

I took a deep breath. "Where do you want to sit, Theo?"

Theo gave me a small smile. "You choose."

"Let's take the two desks under the window," I said, and we walked over to our new seats.

28

Ma had to take time off work to come to portfolio night later that week. We met at school, in the foyer, and she asked where we should go first.

"Let's go to my Spanish class," I said, and soon we were sitting next to each other in front of Mrs. Quezada, who listened to me explain the assignment to Ma.

"Interesting," Ma said. "So what's your new holiday?"

I handed her the poster. Ma studied it, and Mrs. Quezada said, "I didn't know that Wren had lost her father. This is very touching, and I'm sure you two will commemorate the sad event together."

Ma kept her head down, looking at the poster much longer than necessary.

Mrs. Quezada pulled out a sheet and pushed it on the table between us. "This is the comment sheet, Mrs. Kaiser," she said. "I'd appreciate it if you would leave a comment about Wren's work."

Ma had to clear her throat before she said, "Yes, no problem."

While she scribbled something on the sheet, I saw red blotches forming on her neck. Then she got up and very politely said goodbye to Mrs. Quezada. As she walked out of the room, I noticed she was holding herself up much straighter and stiffer than usual.

I hurried after her, but once Ma crossed the hallway, she ran right down the stairs and out through the main door. I caught up with her in the parking lot.

I expected her to yell at me. But she didn't yell.

"I can't do it," Ma said quietly. "I cannot talk about him."

When she looked at me, I could see she wasn't angry. Instead, there was something in her eyes that I hadn't seen before. She was hurt.

* * *

In bed that night, I couldn't stop thinking about the pain I had seen in Ma's face as she'd held the poster. I'd wanted to hurt her back, and it had worked. But now I tossed and turned, unable to fall asleep.

By the time Ma came home from her shift at the diner, I was still awake. I heard the water running in the bathroom, followed by the toilet flushing. Ma's bed squeaked as she lay down. And then, quietly, I heard her sob.

I pulled the pillow over my head.

29

"You guys didn't stay long at portfolio night," Theo said the next morning.

"My mother had to get back to work," I lied. I didn't want to talk about the poster.

"Are you okay?"

I nodded. "Yes." But I knew he could tell I was lying.

Thankfully, Theo let it go. "Want to go to the pond after school?" he asked.

I nodded again, feeling grateful.

* * *

Once we got to the pond I told him what was going on.

"So you made this poster because your mother had to sell your dad's car," Theo said.

"Yes," I said. "And also because she never talks to me about my dad."

"Hmm," Theo said. "So now you're angry at her."

"I am," I said. "How could she do this to me? That was the last thing we had of his."

"Your mother is probably mad too," he said.

"But she's mad at my dad, and he didn't do anything," I said. "That's different."

"Have you ever wondered why she's so mad?" Theo asked.

I shook my head. "Isn't it obvious? She's mad because he died and left her with no money."

"Maybe there's something else," he suggested.

"Like what?"

Theo shrugged. "I don't know. Maybe he did something before he died."

"What would he have done?"

"I don't know," Theo said. "You could ask her."

"I'm not asking her anything ever again. I'm done talking to her," I said. "I hardly even see her, and it's better this way."

Just then a pine siskin appeared in a tree. Theo snapped a few photos.

"It belongs to the finch family," I said when he showed them to me. "See the yellowish tint on the feathers? This one's a male." We noted the sighting in our journals, and I tried to draw the bird but erased my attempt right away.

"Is there a rule that you have to add drawings to your observations?" Theo asked. He now also had a bird journal but only wrote down descriptions and names of birds we saw.

"My dad told me there should be drawings in a bird journal," I said.

"I think I might just paste photos in mine. I really can't draw."

"My dad said that you get better with practice," I told him.

"I have a second digital camera. It's a little older and slower, but the zoom is good. You could have it," Theo offered.

I shook my head. "Thanks, but I don't need a camera."

Theo put his camera down and turned to me. "How did your dad actually die?"

I held my breath. I hadn't told anyone.

But then I told Theo.

I told him about the terrible day of waiting. About the phone call from search and rescue. About Ma burning Dad's papers. About driving up I-75 all the way from Georgia but never talking.

And then I cried.

When the sobbing stopped, I felt empty but also better. "Don't look at me," I said, burying my face in my hands. "I look like a puff fish."

Theo had listened to me quietly. Now he pulled a pack of tissues from his pocket and offered me one. His eyes stayed straight ahead. "I'm not looking," he said. "And they're actually called puffer fish."

I blew my nose. The tissue smelled like pencil shavings.

"That must have been hard not to have a body," he said after a while. "Did you have some kind of memorial service?"

I shook my head.

"You should ask the guy at the garage if he still has the car. If he does, you could go and at least say a proper goodbye to the old car."

I nodded. *Thank you, Theo.*

30

I didn't see Dad's old Volvo among the cars parked next to the office of Karl's Auto Repair when I biked over the next afternoon. The garage was open, and Karl, a stocky man in dark red overalls with his name embroidered on the bib, stood in front of a truck with an opened hood.

"Your mother's Volvo?" he asked when I inquired. "The blue one? Why do you need to know where it is?"

"I forgot something in the glove compartment," I lied.

"Hmm." Karl frowned. "I sold it to Randle. But his junkyard isn't far. You can get there on your bike. Follow 7 Mile Road. You can't miss it. Left-hand side."

* * *

Karl was right. It didn't take long for me to get there. A self-painted sign pointed me toward *Randle's Junkyard — Where Cars Come to Die.*

Where cars come to die . . . ? Was that supposed to be witty? It wasn't.

Scattered across the grass to the left and right of the gravel driveway stood sculptures that had been welded together from rusty auto parts — most of them human-like creatures on two legs with reflectors on hubcaps for faces. Others were oversized flowers. The largest one was a giant metal bird made from mufflers. Next to it stood a sheep, its coat consisting of spark plugs.

I reached a yard filled with old cars. Some stood on cement blocks, their tires removed. Corrosion had eaten a rusty lace on the bottom of the front door of a blue sedan. A yellow Mazda was missing its front doors and a right rear fender.

This really was *where cars come to die,* I realized.

Behind the cars, there was a shack with a sign above the door that said *Office.* I entered. Above the desk, next to the door, hung a corkboard covered with bills. A large poster of a sitting Buddha, smiling a serene smile, covered the opposite wall. Through the open back door, I saw a garage full of shelves filled with car parts.

The wind was picking up now, and the sky had darkened in the west. I went back outside and walked around the shack and saw a red-painted wooden cabin set in a well-kept garden. The driveway was empty, indicating that whoever lived there probably wasn't home.

I scanned another row of cars to the right, near the trees. There was our Volvo.

I walked over and tried the door — it was unlocked, and I slid into the backseat. I let my hand glide over the seat cover, caressing the burn mark Dad had said was already there when he bought the car.

I inhaled the smell. It felt so good to be in the car. I leaned back, closed my eyes, and took deep breaths. Raindrops started drumming on the hood and roof. I fell asleep to their soft rhythm, and soon I was dreaming of driving along a sun-drenched road in Georgia with Dad. We were on the way to the coast on a birding expedition. We passed trees covered with Spanish moss, while Dad sang one of his silly songs. It was so bright outside that I had to shield my eyes from the sun. We laughed.

Suddenly a man's voice interrupted my memory. "Who are you?"

I woke up, startled. It was raining hard, and the man who'd spoken was standing outside, holding a jacket over his head. He was about Ma's age and tall, with dark, shoulder-length hair. He was dressed in jeans and an oil-stained T-shirt.

"Were you sleeping in there?" he asked.

"No, I was just, like, sitting in it," I said, still groggy. I climbed out of the car.

"You all right?" The man looked concerned.

"I'm fine," I said. "Who are you?"

"Randle," he said, offering his hand. "I own this place."

"Wren," I said, shaking his hand.

"Are you a runaway or something?" he asked.

"No, no. I'm no runaway," I said. "I wasn't looking for a place to sleep. That used to be my dad's car. I was just saying goodbye to it."

"Come on. I live over there," Randle said, pointing to the cabin on the other side of the lot. "We need to get out of this weather."

I followed him through the rain, but when we reached the driveway, I hesitated. He was a stranger after all, and I was about to go into his house. He caught my glance. Above the entrance to his house, several clotheslines displayed small flags of different colors.

"Those are Tibetan prayer flags," Randle said as he opened the door. "They promote wisdom, strength, compassion, and peace."

I decided to follow him inside — after all, how bad could someone with Tibetan prayer flags be? He led me into a large, sparsely furnished room with a kitchen counter at one end and a living room sofa with a chair and coffee table at the other.

"I'll get a towel," he said and disappeared into the back.

I glanced around the room. This didn't look like the home of a junkyard guy. A bookshelf held a few art books and several crime novels. I recognized some of the titles Ma had read before she'd switched to romance. On an antique sideboard, a stone Buddha looked sternly ahead, one hand up, his palm toward me.

Just then Randle returned and handed me a towel.

I dried my hair and dabbed the nape of my neck. "Are you a Buddhist?" I asked.

"Try to be," Randle said. He walked over to the kitchen counter. "Want a smoothie? I usually have one this time of day."

"Sure."

I watched him take out a cup of berries and carrots from the refrigerator and noticed a thick scar that snaked around his wrist like a bracelet. He peeled a banana and threw the fruit into the blender, poured almond milk on top of it, and pressed the start button. When the noise stopped, he poured the foamy liquid into two glasses.

There was an envelope on the counter, and I read the addressee.

"Randle Redbird, that's your name?" I asked.

He nodded. "Yes, it's a Chippewa Indian name."

"I thought you were a Buddhist."

"I am," he said. "I'm also part Chippewa Indian." He motioned for me to sit down at the kitchen table and handed me one of the glasses. "'To keep the body in good health is a duty,' the Buddha said." He lifted his glass in my direction.

I took a sip of mine. "It's good," I said.

Randle pulled out a rubber band to tie his hair into a ponytail, and I saw burn marks on the underside of his arms. I wondered how he'd gotten all those scars.

"So you're sad to see the old Volvo go, hmm?"

I nodded. With his hair back, Randle looked handsome, like a rustic Keanu Reeves.

"Gotta say, though, your old man didn't take too good care of it."

"What do you mean?" I asked.

"The motor hasn't seen any new oil for a long time, and the tires had almost no more tread. Didn't get a lot of love and tenderness, this one."

"My ma's been driving it now for three months," I said. "We came here all the way from Georgia."

"Divorce?" Randle asked.

I shook my head. "Death."

"Your ma got rid of the car before you had time to let it go?"

"Mm-hmm." I nodded.

"The Buddha said that life and death are inseparable," Randle told me. "He wants us to learn to let go."

I put my glass down on the counter. This Buddha talk was getting on my nerves. "I should get going," I said.

"I know losing someone you love is hard," he added. "My favorite foster dad died when I was twelve."

"You were in foster care?" I asked.

Randle nodded. "For most of my life before I was old enough to live on my own."

"What about your real parents?"

He shrugged. "I never met my dad, and my mother left me on the steps of the Salvation Army as a baby."

I didn't say anything. Now would have been a good time to ask about the scars, but I didn't dare.

"You know, if you want me to, I could fix up the Volvo for one last ride," Randle offered. "That way you could say goodbye."

"Thanks for the smoothie," I said. "And thanks for the offer. I'll think about it."

"You bet," he said. "Nice meeting you. And I mean it. I won't take it apart for a few days. If you wanna do it, just drop by."

31

At school the next day I told Theo about Randle and his offer. "I think he's some kind of artist," I said. "And also a Buddhist. He lives in an almost empty cabin and throws around all sorts of wise sayings. And he has all these scars on his arms."

"Sounds like an interesting guy."

"Yeah . . . I'm not sure about him."

"Are you going to go on that last drive with him?" Theo asked.

"I don't know," I replied. "What do you think? Should I do it?"

"I think you shouldn't go alone," Theo said. "It could be dangerous."

"Yeah...I was wondering if I should have followed him into his house yesterday," I said. "But he *is* a Buddhist — all about peace and harmony, you know."

"Well, you never know actually," Theo said.

"True," I said. "I do trust him, though. But you could come with me anyway. I'm sure he wouldn't mind."

Theo nodded. "Sure. I'd like to meet this guy."

* * *

After school, we pedaled to Randle's Junkyard. I introduced the two and told Randle that I'd like to take that drive.

"No problem. I can get the Volvo in shape for a last spin right away," Randle said. "I'm glad you brought a friend."

While he was getting the Volvo ready, Theo and I walked around and looked at the sculptures. When it was time, we got into the backseat of the car, and Theo asked, "How did you get the scar under your arm?"

"My mother burned me when I was a baby."

"By accident?"

Randle shook his head. "No. She was drunk, and I was screaming. She thought it would shut me up." He then pointed to the thick scar around his wrist. "This one is from the first foster family I lived with. We had an argument and my foster dad settled it with a knife. I didn't stay there very long."

The motor sputtered when Randle turned the key in the ignition.

"Old Volv's got the hiccups," he said, patting the dashboard affectionately. "He'll be all right."

Soon we drove out of his lot, and Randle turned onto 7 Mile Road. He looked at me in the rearview mirror. "Are you okay?"

I nodded. The truth was, it felt strange to be in the car. Part of me wanted to be alone. I waited for the cloud to wrap around me, but something had changed. I wasn't alone.

The car sputtered again, and Randle said, "Come on, Old Man Volvo. Pull yourself together for Wren's last ride."

"Thank you for doing this," I said.

"No problem," Randle said. "But this old motor is truly on its last leg. It'll gobble up the oil I gave it, and

I won't be able to resuscitate it for much longer than this ride."

I leaned against the backrest and tried to think of Dad. But the only picture I had in my mind was of Randle as a baby being burned by his mother. I tried to concentrate on Dad, wanting to bring up some image of us in the car. When had we last driven in the car together? But I couldn't replay a happy memory.

Instead, I thought of Randle having a fight with his foster dad. It had to be so terrible that it ended in scars. Then I remembered a day Dad had driven me to school, and we'd argued. It had been a stupid fight over a dumb thing, and I'd gotten out and slammed the door. I still felt bad about it now.

"Music?" Randle asked, holding up two CDs. "You want sad or funky?"

"Sad."

Randle pushed one of the discs into the console, and a moment later, a raspy man's voice came out of the speakers.

"Who's that?" Theo asked.

"Leonard Cohen," Randle said. "One of the best."

I relaxed as I listened. It sounded as if he was performing a slow poem to music. He spoke the words more than he sang them. There was this pain in his voice, but I found it soothing. And I loved the refrain:

Ring the bell that still can ring
Forget your perfect offering
There is a crack, a crack in everything
That's how the light gets in.

32

"Feeling better now?" Randle asked once we were back at the house.

"I don't know," I said. "Maybe a little. Thank you, again, for doing this."

"Letting go is very hard," he said. "Believe me, I know." As he spoke, he glanced over at a pile of boxes next to the hallway door.

"What's all that?" Theo asked.

"That's my mother's stuff. I cleared out her house."

"I thought you said your mother left you at the Salvation Army when you were a baby. Isn't that true?" I asked.

"Oh yes," Randle said. "I actually only met her recently. The foster care system opened the files they had on me, and I learned who she was. We actually didn't live that far apart all these years."

"What was it like when you met her?" I asked.

"Well," Randle said, "it is kind of sad. She has Alzheimer's, and her memory is fuzzy. So pretty much right after we met, I had to help her move into an old folks' home with special care."

"I'm sorry," I said.

Randle nodded. "Yeah, it's sad. She's not even that old. Early onset, they call it."

"What about these photos?" Theo asked, peering into a small box on top of the pile.

"I think my father took those. He was into photography."

"May I look at them?" Theo asked politely.

"Sure, go ahead."

Theo quietly flipped through them for a few minutes. "These are mostly bird photos," he said. "Some of them look like they were taken at Pete's Pond."

"My ma loves birds. That's one of the few things I've learned about her since we met," Randle said. "And from the looks of it, my dad did too. But how do you know that's Pete's Pond?"

"Look here," Theo said, pointing to one photo. "This is a panoramic view of the pond with the birch trunks in the back."

"It looks pretty much the same now as it did then," I added.

"How do you guys know that place?" Randle asked.

"We go there to watch birds," I said. "Right now, we're trying to save it since they want to use the area to expand the Pyramid Landfill. We're collecting signatures."

"Oh, that's cool," Randle said. "Can I sign?"

I nodded. "We'll bring the petition next time we see you."

"Who's this?" Theo asked, pulling out a photo of a man and a woman.

"My parents," Randle answered.

"I thought you said you'd never met your dad," I said.

"I didn't. He died before I was born. I put that photo aside 'cause I wanted to bring it to my ma." Randle handed Theo the photograph. "It's in bad shape, though. See?"

"It needs to be restored," Theo said.

"Can you do that?" I asked, looking over at him.

Theo shrugged. "I could try."

"I'd love for you to take a shot at it," Randle said. "Ma sure would be over the moon if we could show it to her with the both of them actually visible."

"Aren't you angry at your ma for giving you up?" I asked. It was hard to imagine that he could have forgiven his mother for doing that.

"She had her reasons for not wanting a baby," Randle said. "She couldn't have taken care of me."

"But you ended up with terrible foster parents. Look at your wrist. That wouldn't have happened if she hadn't abandoned you," I said.

"There's no point in holding on to anger or resentment. As the Buddha said, 'Don't be loyal to your suffering.' With things the way they are now, my ma and I just have to make the best out of the time we have left."

Randle paused for a moment. "Actually," he continued, "you always should make the best out of the time you have. 'Live in joy,' as the Buddha said."

33

"Soon we might not be able to come here anymore," I said to Theo when we met at the pond a few days later. "It'll all be gone. Randle would probably say that the Buddha tells us not to cling to anything." I threw my hands up in the air and called out, "Let it all go, your pain, your fears, your wetlands . . ."

Theo laughed. "I don't think the Buddha would say you should bury all these things in a landfill. The Buddha would probably be in favor of recycling, like Randle. He reuses most of the car parts."

"I wish he wouldn't say all this stuff about Buddha. 'Let go of your suffering' and 'Don't cling to your bad feelings' and so on. I can't stand how he rubs that in all the time."

"Don't you think it's true?" Theo asked.

"I don't know. But he sounds like those little sayings that people print on calendars with cheesy kitten photos," I said.

"It's not cheesy," Theo said. "He's certainly forgiven his mother. Imagine, she burns him, hurts him in all kinds of ways, and then gives him away. And yet, he finds her and takes care of her. That's awesome."

I fought the urge to roll my eyes. It seemed everybody around me thought that Randle and his Buddha were saints. The day before, when I'd told Mr. Leroy about him, he'd said, "He's a Buddhist Chippewa Indian who looks like Keanu Reeves? It sounds like you met one of the most interesting characters in Pyramid. I hope you told him about my store in case he needs some whey powder for his smoothies."

"Of course I did," I'd said, smiling.

"Good, I'd like to meet that man."

"He's really into Buddhism and keeps quoting *the Buddha*." I'd rolled my eyes.

"Don't make fun of that," Mr. Leroy had said. "Buddhism is a great philosophy. It's about being peaceful and not wanting too many material things and living in the moment."

"Are you living in the moment?" I'd asked him.

Mr. Leroy had laughed. "You're asking hard questions today, Wren. This Randle has got you thinking." And after a short pause, he'd continued, "I guess it would be good if I could live in the moment. But like everyone else, I worry about the future and obsess about the past. I admire people who can live in the *now*." He put imaginary quotation marks around that word in the air. "But all these wise things are easier said than done."

* * *

Later in the afternoon, Theo and I brought Randle the restored photo. I could tell he was touched when he saw the black-and-white picture of his parents.

"Oh Lordy," he said, studying the image. "It's like new. I only drove you around in an old car, and you're giving me this great gift. You guys are something else."

"It was really nice of you to take me on that ride," I said. I handed him another album of pictures too. "We also brought these bird photos for your mother. You told us she likes birds. Theo took them for a school report."

"Wow, man! Thank you! You should go pro with this, Theo!" Randle exclaimed, looking through the album. "These are really good. You've got the eye."

"Thanks," Theo said, his ears turning red, giving away how proud he felt.

"I'd love for you to take some photos of my sculptures," Randle continued. "I had a guy come by who wanted to offer some of them to a gallery. He left his card and said I should send him some shots. I'd pay you for it."

"I'm happy to take some photos of your sculptures," Theo said. "But I don't want any money for them."

Randle opened his arms, and in a quick movement, pressed us both against his chest. When he let go, I could tell Theo was as embarrassed as I was. We both stepped farther away than necessary.

"I'm still looking through this shoe box, trying to find some other photos my mom might like," Randle said. "Most of them are of birds and trees. My dad was really into nature photography."

"Why don't you take the whole box?" I asked.

"The doctor said that it would be better not to overwhelm her with memories," Randle said. "So I only bring her one or two each week. Some of these photos are weird." He pointed to three black-and-white images. "There are several of a turtle shell my dad apparently found interesting."

"That looks just like the shell we found," Theo said. "It has the same kind of holes in it."

"There's a date on the back," I said. *"Pete's Pond, May 1971."*

"You found a shell like this at the same place? That's interesting," Randle said.

"Maybe we could ask your mother about it," Theo suggested.

Randle nodded. "I think you guys should come with me anyway when I give the photos to her."

I looked at Theo, who nodded. "Sure," we said in unison.

34

In the reception area of the Golden Acres Retirement Home, it smelled like cabbage and bleach. We crossed a room next to the foyer where four old women sat in their wheelchairs like fragile dolls, slightly bent over, their heads turned toward the flat screen TV that was mounted above a fireplace.

I couldn't help staring at their wrinkled, gaunt faces, wondering if it was their white hair and the faded colors of their clothes that made them all look alike, or if it was something else.

We passed a window in the hallway that opened into the garden. Outside, I saw Ma pushing an old woman in a wheelchair. I hadn't expected to see her here. Monday was her day off, but maybe she'd switched her shifts. I paused and watched her park the wheelchair next to a bench. Then she sat down and took out a book. She said something that made the old woman smile. Then Ma began to read to her. The old woman reached out and touched Ma's knee. Ma looked up and smiled at her, then continued to read.

It gave me a pang to see such a tender expression on Ma's face. She never looked like that at home.

"Who's that lovely lady you are looking at?" Randle asked, standing behind me.

"My mother," I said. "She works here."

"You want to go outside and introduce us?" Randle asked.

I shook my head. "I'd rather not. I didn't tell her that I tracked down the Volvo and that you drove me around in it. We're not talking very much right now."

"Oh, I see," Randle said, raising his eyebrows. "I sense some mother-daughter conflict here."

"Indeed," I said. "A big one."

Thankfully, Randle let it go at that, and we made our way to his mother's quarters. Mrs. Redbird's room was small but light-filled. She sat by the window in a wingback chair. Her spidery fingers clasped the armrest like a bird holds on to a branch. "These are your friends from school?" she asked, looking at us doubtfully.

"No, Mother," Randle said patiently. "This is Theo and Wren. They brought you something." He held out the black-and-white photo.

Mrs. Redbird's eyes glazed over as she gently touched the photo of her husband. "Oh, Edward," she whispered.

Randle threw us a thankful look, then walked over to his mother and gave her a hug. In the car he'd told us that his mother was so confused at times that he didn't know if she would even recognize his father.

I thought of the scars on his arm as I looked at the two of them hugging. Theo was right. It was awesome of Randle to take care of his mother now even after she'd abandoned him.

"Are we going somewhere?" Mrs. Redbird asked.

"No, mother," Randle said. "We aren't going anywhere. But I have another photo. Edward took pictures of a turtle shell. Do you remember anything about it?"

Mrs. Redbird looked at the photo and said, "Edward liked pork roast. He . . ." Her voice trailed off, and suddenly she looked at us with an empty stare.

"We also brought you some bird photos in color," Randle said, placing our album in her lap. "Theo took those."

Randle's mother studied the photos slowly. "Edward had the fever," she said, looking out of the window. "We gave him herbs and medicine, but the cough wouldn't stop." Then her eyes teared up, and she sobbed.

"Oh, Ma," Randle comforted her. "That's all long passed." He dabbed her face with a tissue and pointed to another photo. "You know that bird?"

Mrs. Redbird stopped crying and pursed her lips. After a moment, she whistled the short song of a chickadee, making us smile.

* * *

"Now I'm kind of curious about this shell," Randle said, when we were back in his car. "You guys know the librarian, right? Maybe we could go and check with her."

Theo and I agreed, but when we arrived at the library, Mrs. Carter, the library assistant, told us that Mrs. Russo had just stepped out.

"What should we Google to find out about the turtle shell?" I asked when we sat down at the computer in the library reading room. I noticed an issue of *Aviator* was still on the magazine rack and quickly looked away. But this time, it didn't trigger terrible thoughts about Dad.

"Just enter *turtle shell with holes, Upper Peninsula, Michigan*," Theo suggested.

I followed his instructions, and several links quickly appeared on the screen: *Turtle Shell Construction Company, box turtle fact sheet, turtle diseases.*

I shook my head. "Nothing fits."

We tried a few more times but couldn't come up with anything useful. When Mrs. Russo returned, we were all grateful. Theo and I introduced Randle and explained what we were looking for.

"And you think they're box turtles?" Mrs. Russo asked.

"That's what they look like," Theo said.

"My father used to take photos at the pond, just like these kids do now," Randle added. "I think it's curious that he found the same kind of shell, about forty years ago, at the same place."

"And they each have two pairs of holes drilled in them," I said. "Isn't that strange?"

"It is," Mrs. Russo agreed. "We could log on to one of our databases; that will exclude all of the commercial sites." She sat next to us, and her fingers flew across the keyboard. "I can't get anything offhand," she said after a while. "Why don't you leave the shell with me, and give me a few days. I'll see what I can find."

35

Ma and I hadn't really talked since portfolio night. Well, to be fair, we hadn't talked much before that either. But now it was just "pass me the salt" or "did you finish your homework?" or "I'm running a wash with dark clothes, do you have anything to add?"

I was fine with that and didn't mind the super quiet dinners. The strange thing was, despite the silence, the cloud had gotten smaller. It wasn't that I didn't think of Dad anymore. It was more that when I *did* think of him, it hurt less.

Maybe there were stages of grieving after all, and I had reached another one. Or maybe I was on top of a peak on a zigzag graph of healing, and soon I would drop down again to a place where it hurt more. Or maybe there was only enough space inside my heart for one bad feeling at a time and being so mad at Ma had washed out the pain about Dad.

On Saturday morning, Ma didn't have to work. When I heard her leave the apartment early that morning, I figured it was to avoid me, but she came back soon with a bag full of fruit, whole wheat bread, and artisanal cheese.

"This must have cost a fortune," I said.

"Now don't worry about the cost," she said as she unpacked the groceries. "I got an employee discount at Mr. Leroy's."

"You went to Mr. Leroy's?"

"I did," she said. "What a nice man, and he's full of praise for you."

"What did he say about me?" I asked.

"Just that you're so kind and helpful," she said, getting out a juicer that I didn't even know we owned. "He told me you like these." She held up a bag of my favorite coconut granola bars.

"I do," I said. "Thanks."

"I have a new job, too," Ma said.

"A third job?" I asked, watching her squeeze oranges. "When will you have time for that?"

"Well, it's actually an addition to the job I already have at the nursing home," Ma said. "There's this old lady whose daughter was looking for someone to read to her. So she hired me to read during lunch and after my shifts."

Now I knew why we'd seen Ma the other day. "You get paid for that?"

Ma nodded. "I do. Handsomely. I've already put two hundred dollars into the savings account." From the way she looked at me, I could tell she was checking my reaction.

"That's nice," I said.

"What's new in your life?" she asked.

I shrugged. "Nothing."

"Something must be happening," Ma urged.

"Everything is fine," I said.

"I saw your petition at Mr. Leroy's," she continued, trying to make conversation. "That's something new you could tell me about."

She clearly wasn't going to let this go. "Theo and I are going to the farmer's market today to collect signatures," I said. "State Senator Larsson is scheduled to go through

BE LIGHT LIKE A BIRD

the aisles to talk to voters, and that's when we'll show him our petition. It's going to change everything."

"How so?"

"A team of television reporters will be there, following him around. When we talk to him, we'll pull out our posters, demanding that Pete's Pond be saved, and maybe they'll put it on the evening news."

"That's a great idea," Ma said, handing me the juice.

I took it. I could tell she was trying to be extra nice. But one fresh-pressed juice wouldn't make up for what had happened between us.

36

"This is really nice of you to help us," I said to Theo's father later that morning. He'd already carried a table and easel from his car to our spot at the farmer's market.

"You're welcome," Mr. Guttner replied.

I could see the resemblance between Theo and his dad. Mr. Guttner had the same bushy eyebrows and dark blue eyes as Theo. He also didn't seem to pay much attention to his clothes — his jeans were two inches too short, and there was a moth hole in the brown sweater vest he wore under a vintage rain jacket.

When his dad went back to the car to get the chairs, Theo turned to me and said, "I can't believe it. When I told him about the petition, he was all excited and called it a 'true civil action' and wanted to help."

"Maybe it reminds him of his days in politics," I suggested as we fastened the photographs onto the easel and taped the poster to the top. The words *Save Pete's Pond— Sign Our Petition Here!* stood out in large green letters.

"Maybe," Theo said. "Whatever the reason, I'm just glad he came."

In front of the town hall, workers had assembled a platform for the senator to give his speech. Next to it stood a white van with a satellite dish on its roof and the words *9 & 10 News — Northern Michigan's News Leader* printed in large blue letters on the side. A woman in a red pantsuit got out and arranged her hair, looking at her reflection in the side window. I recognized her from the local news. As she primped, a young man in a lumberjack shirt set up a camera in front of the platform.

Theo's dad returned with the chairs and wanted a coffee, and I walked over to the coffee shop to order one black coffee to go. While I waited in front of the counter, the woman in the pantsuit entered, followed by the cameraman. She looked at the menu and complained, "I told you that there wouldn't be anything healthy to eat here. Everything is deep-fried or made of carbs."

"I think you should try a pasty," the cameraman said, smiling. "That's good, hearty food." He pointed to a plate under a glass cover. "It's a type of turnover filled with meat, potatoes, and some veggies. Famous dish here in the U.P."

The reporter shook her head. "That doesn't sound very good."

"I can show you where you can buy a healthy breakfast," I offered.

"Where's that?" she asked.

"The local health food store has a booth at the farmer's market," I said. "I can take you there."

"It can't be any worse than here," she said with a sigh. She turned to the cameraman. "Are you coming?"

"No," he said. "I'll have the greasy local food!"

I led the way to Mr. Leroy's booth. He had decorated his stall with a jug of wild flowers on a red-and-white checkered tablecloth and built a little pyramid of small jars filled with honey and jam next to a basket of different granola mixes. He was cutting thick slices from a dark loaf of bread when we arrived.

"This looks like real bread," the woman said. "What are you putting on it?"

"I have goat cheese from a creamery in Mackinaw, and I'll sprinkle it with watercress," Mr. Leroy replied.

"Mmm. That sounds good," she said. "I'll have one of those."

"Aren't you Kelly Gustafson?" Mr. Leroy asked as he prepared her sandwich. "I've seen you on TV."

"Yes," she said. "That's me. We're here to follow the senator around. Not much else going on around here, I suppose."

"Well, I wouldn't say that," Mr. Leroy said. "You talk to Wren here, and she can tell you about a very important cause she's fighting for in our community."

"What's that about, Wren?" she asked.

"There's a wetland area surrounding a pond — Pete's Pond — on the outskirts of Pyramid with lots of birds," I explained. "But now the owner of the landfill, which is next to the wetland, wants to drain the pond. Maybe you could come with me to our stall. A friend of mine and I have —"

Just then Ms. Gustafson's cell phone rang and interrupted me in midsentence. She answered, and after just a few seconds, she snapped the phone shut. "The senator is here. I have to go." She paid for the sandwich, and before she left, turned to me. "Thanks for showing me the way to a good breakfast! I really appreciate it! Here's my card in case you have anything interesting to report."

* * *

"The senator has arrived," Theo's father said when I returned with the coffee. "I think we should get ready."

"Here are the clipboards with the signature sheets," Theo said, handing me one.

"Now all we need are people to sign and the senator to come by," I said.

"And the weather has to stay dry," Theo added. "It's supposed to rain later. That wouldn't be good for our plan."

Soon after, Senator Larsson climbed onto the stage and went behind the microphone and began his speech. He praised his connection to the Upper Peninsula and promised new employment opportunities.

"This is boring," Theo said.

"I agree. But look over there," I said, pointing. A woman was buying tomatoes at the stall next to ours. "We should ask her to sign the petition."

"Go ahead," Theo said.

I quickly walked over. "Would you like to sign our petition?" I asked, holding out the clipboard. "We're asking the township not to allow the expansion of the landfill. We want Pete's Pond to be protected."

"Sure," the woman said. "I heard about your project at the library. It's great that young people like you are standing up for something like this." She signed her name, returned the pen with a smile, and said, "Good luck!"

"Thank you," I said. I walked back over to Theo.

"There you go," Theo said. "The first signature, and we've only been here a half hour."

"That was easier than I thought," I said. Just then, I heard a familiar voice behind me and turned around to see Ma standing there. "What are you doing here?" I asked.

"I thought you might like some help," Ma said. "You could give me one of these clipboards, and I could start asking people for their signatures." She turned to Mr. Guttner, acting as if we were just any normal mother-daughter pair. "You must be Theo's dad. I'm Wren's mother."

"Nice to meet you," Mr. Guttner said.

"Can I have one of these?" Ma pointed to the clipboards with the signature sheets.

"Sure," Mr. Guttner replied.

Ma got right to work. She stopped an elderly couple a few stalls down, and after only a quick talk, they both signed. Next, she approached a woman with a stroller, who also signed right away.

"Your ma is a natural," Mr. Guttner commented.

Theo looked at me, and I shrugged. I knew Ma was doing this to get on my good side, but I couldn't be entirely upset. She'd already gotten several signatures for us.

Suddenly Carrie was standing in front of our booth leading a small poodle on a leash. "Hi," she said.

"Oh, hello," I said. "You got a dog." I felt awkward and was glad I could bend down to pat the dog's head.

"Her name is Bonnie," Carrie said. Bonnie was eager to greet me; she jumped up and licked my hand.

"She's very cute," I replied. "So you didn't have to take a dog from the shelter after all."

Carrie looked at the posters and didn't say anything.

"I guess you don't want to sign this," I said. "It's a petition against the landfill expansion."

"No, I won't sign," Carrie snapped, her voice sharp. "The landfill expansion is a done deal. I don't even know why you're wasting everybody's time."

"Well, a lot of people don't think it's a waste of time," I said calmly. "It's worth a try, in my opinion."

Carrie looked at Theo, who was handing a pen to a young man with a ponytail.

"Suit yourselves," Carrie said. "Come on, Bonnie. Let's go." She tugged on the dog's leash and stomped away.

A little farther down the aisle, Ma stopped Carrie and held the clipboard with the petition up. Carrie shook her head and walked on.

37

"The senator has finished talking," Theo said, pointing toward the stage. "Now he'll start walking the aisles."

Sure enough, the senator left the stage, followed by his wife and the TV crew, and approached the first stall. He shook hands with its vendor. Next, he stopped at a table selling homemade candles. Again, he shook hands with a customer, a wide grin on his face.

"That's what politicians do best," Mr. Guttner said. "Glad-handing!"

I frowned. "If he continues this slowly, he won't reach us before noon."

Just then Ms. Gustafson, followed by the cameraman, stepped into the senator's path. I let out a loud sigh. "Now the TV lady interviews him," I said.

"But they're standing right in front of Mr. Leroy's stall. So he'll be on TV for sure," Theo said.

"I want him to hurry," I said, glancing up at the sky, where dark clouds had gathered. "It's starting to sprinkle, and there are more clouds coming."

"How's it going?" we heard someone ask.

All three of us turned around, and there was Mrs. Russo, standing in front of our booth with a basket on her arm. She lifted the cloth on her basket.

"I'm sorry I can't stay, but I brought you some snacks," she said. "These are cinnamon rolls. I made them myself." She turned to Theo's dad. "Would you like one?"

"Sure," he said. When their eyes met, he blushed.

Theo and I each took a roll and thanked Mrs. Russo. While we chewed the delicious pastries, I stepped away from our table, tugging Theo's sleeve so he would follow.

"Did you see how your dad and Mrs. Russo looked at each other?" I whispered.

"I know," Theo said, smiling. "Unbelievable."

I glanced around. The senator was only one aisle away from us now. He wasn't stopping at every stall, but he did visit every row. In my mind, I played the sequence as we had planned it. We would involve the senator in a conversation. Theo's father would show him the petition and ask him to sign it. Theo would point to the photos, and when the TV cameras were close enough, I would hold up my poster behind him.

At that moment, the wind had picked up. Thick raindrops began to fall onto our table.

"Let's cover the signature lists," Mr. Guttner said, pulling a plastic sheet over our table just before the rain really came down.

"This isn't supposed to happen," Theo said.

As an aid held a large umbrella over his head, the senator hurried toward a black limousine. In the distance, Ma tried to talk to a woman who'd sought shelter from the downpour under the awning of the potato stall, but the woman shook her head no.

Theo's father pointed to the motorcade. "They're leaving!" he said. "I'm sorry, guys."

"What are we going to do now?" Theo asked.

"We have eighty-nine signatures," I said, glancing at the list. "I don't know how many my mother has. But we can't give up now. What if we actually attend the meeting instead of just submitting the signed petition to the office? Then Mr. Zusack has to look us in the eye when he votes to destroy Pete's Pond."

"That will hardly make any difference to him," Theo said.

"We have to try. I read in the paper that the township board is meeting on Friday, and I think we should be there. We have more than eighty-nine signatures. That means that more than eighty-nine people are on our side. And if we hand over the petition at a public meeting, it'll get more attention."

"Even one hundred isn't even close to the majority of people who live here," Theo said.

"But the people who signed also gave us their phone numbers," I pointed out. "Would you help me call them and ask them to come?"

Theo nodded.

"Wren has the right idea," Theo's dad said with a smile. "She's going to be the queen of civil action."

38

At home Ma and I hung our clothes up to dry. I put on a sweater, and when I came back into the kitchen, I could smell hot cocoa. Ma handed me a cup. She had made one for herself too.

"Thanks for coming out and helping with the signatures today," I said as we sat down at the kitchen table.

"You're welcome," Ma said. "I'm sorry the senator left before you could show your petition to him. Perhaps you should consider writing to him."

I nodded. "We won't give up the fight. We'll go to the township meeting and present the petition in person. You know what Dad used to say: 'It ain't over until the fat lady sings.' And she hasn't sung yet."

I watched Ma's face carefully as I mentioned Dad. But instead of the usual frown, her face remained neutral. She looked straight at me. I could sense she wanted to talk about something, and a tiny butterfly was tickling the inside of my stomach.

Ma cleared her throat. "I know it wasn't right of me to sell the car without talking to you first," she began. "And I know you needed to talk with me about your dad, and I avoided you. But . . ." She took a breath. "When I went through his things I found out he . . . he cheated on me. Your dad had a girlfriend."

"That is not true." The words shot out of me.

"It is true," Ma said. "There were letters from her. It had been going on for a while — at least two years."

"I don't believe you. Why would they write letters? Everyone sends emails now."

"I couldn't believe it either. I still can't. But I read the letters. He kept them all." Ma paused. "I also found a receipt. Last Thanksgiving, when he told us he was going to his pilot training seminar, he went to a spa with her."

"What's the woman's name?"

"Wren," Ma said, wringing her hands. "I don't think that's important. I didn't want to tell you any of this. I knew it would upset you and —"

"What is the woman's name?" I demanded.

Ma sighed. "Carolyn Ondra — same last name as my first-grade teacher's. She lived in Brookhaven. Her address was on the envelopes I found."

There was a gushing in my ear, like I was standing next to a very loud stream. "It can't be true!" I cried. "You're making this up so that I'll stop loving him. But it won't work. I'll never stop loving Dad, and he would never do something like that."

I got up from the table, pushing my chair back with a loud, angry scrape.

"Hear me out, Wren," Ma said. "He did do it. In several of the most recent letters, she mentioned their plans to live together. He was planning to leave me . . . us. That's why I burned everything."

"None of this is true!" I yelled. "I thought we were going to share our memories of him, talk about the things we did together. Instead, you're making up this big fat lie!"

"Wren, please," Ma begged. "Why would I lie to you?"

"He wouldn't have left us," I said as I hurried toward the door. "How can you even say something like that?"

"Wren!" Ma called after me. "Don't run off. Please! Let's talk about what happened."

"I've wanted to talk for a long time!" I yelled. "But not like this."

39

I jumped on my bike and pedaled to the library. Icy rain pelted down, but I felt hot, like I was drowning in a bubbling mass, boiling in a witch's cauldron. From the public phone in the library lobby, I called the operator. I needed to know if Carolyn Ondra in Brookhaven was a real person. If she had a landline, I would be able to get her number.

As I spoke to the automated operator, I hoped that I wouldn't find a listing in Brookhaven for a woman of that name. That Ma had made it all up. But the mechanical voice announced a number, and with cold hands I wrote it down.

Through the glass doors, I could see Mrs. Russo helping someone at the circulation desk, but I didn't want to talk to anyone right now. My jacket was soaked, and I hadn't put on my rain boots when I'd stormed out of the house, so now my feet were wet. I went to the bathroom and dried my hair under the hand dryer. It was raining too hard to go to the pond, so when I was finished, I sat on the bench in the hallway, trying to calm down.

I just could not believe what Ma had told me. I knew about people having affairs. Mr. Leroy's wife had left him for another man. It happened. But before people split up, they fought a lot and things got ugly. That hadn't happened with Ma and Dad. There hadn't been any sign of trouble — none whatsoever. And even if there had been, when a man left his wife, he also left his child. Dad would never, ever, *ever* have done that.

I found several quarters in my bag. My hands were shivering as I dialed the number I'd written down. It took three rings before a man answered.

"Could I please speak to Carolyn Ondra?" I said.

"Ms. Ondra doesn't live here anymore," he told me. "But she left a forwarding address. Do you have a pen?"

I said yes, and the man rattled off an address in Chicago. This time the operator had no listing. Ms.

Ondra probably only used a cell phone now. If I wanted to talk to her, I'd have to go to Chicago.

* * *

After leaving the library, I decided to stop at Theo's. I couldn't go home. His father wasn't home, and Theo invited me into the kitchen. "You should put your jacket over the radiator to dry," he said as we sat down. "You look upset. What's wrong?"

"I finally talked to my mother. She claims my father had a girlfriend," I began. "But there is no way this is true. She's lying." I had to steady my voice.

"Tell me everything, one thing at a time," Theo said. "And don't forget to breathe."

When I was done telling him what had happened, Theo said, "I don't think it's a good idea to go to Chicago. It'll hurt you to talk to that woman."

"But she might tell me something new about my dad."

"You just learned something new about him. You learned that he wasn't as perfect as you thought he was. I don't think you need to go to Chicago to find out more."

I shook my head. "You don't understand."

"I do understand," Theo said. "But what about your mother? She'll be worried if you don't come home."

"I don't care."

"It's not her fault that your dad had a girlfriend. She's probably hurt too."

"Why didn't she tell me about it before?"

"She tried to tell you now," Theo pointed out. "You ran off."

"Because it *can't* be true!" I exclaimed. "There's no way he wanted to leave us."

"Why would she make it up?" he asked.

"To hurt me," I said. "To make me stop loving him."

Theo shook his head. "If you're honest with yourself, you can't actually deny the woman's existence. By wanting to go to Chicago, you've already acknowledged that she's real. Therefore, you're acting illogically."

"You don't understand," I said again. "It's not a logic problem."

"No, it's a problem of being hurt. Still, that's not a good base for decision making."

I looked at my hands, avoiding Theo's gaze and his advice. "There must be a bus to Chicago."

40

The Indian Trail Motorcoach terminal was near the Studebaker Restaurant. After the rain had stopped, I tried to stay warm by pedaling fast and working up a sweat. Theo hadn't been happy when he couldn't convince me not to look for the woman, but at least he'd agreed to keep quiet.

At the terminal's ticket booth, I learned that the overnight bus to Chicago was leaving that evening at seven o'clock. Ma would be at work, and I would have enough time to go home, change my clothes, and get some money. By the time she realized I was gone, I would be already in Chicago.

On my way back to the apartment, the sun burned through the cloud cover, and a few big puffy clouds sailed high against a deep blue sky. In the sudden sunlight, everything was sparkling, and I felt better now that I had a plan.

I'd just turned onto Easterday Avenue when I saw a dead animal by the side of the road. At first I thought it was a raccoon, but as I came closer, it turned out to be a dog — a small black-and-white terrier, his head resting on the asphalt in a small puddle of blood.

I got off the bike and took my gloves and trowel out of my bag. There were too many houses along the street, so I wouldn't be able to bury the dog right here. When I bent down to pick it up, I saw that it wore a collar with a tin name tag. Engraved on it was the name *Cory* and an address.

My heart sank. Now I would have to bring him to his owner and deliver the terrible news. I imagined myself knocking on the door, holding Cory in my arms. A woman would answer the door, and when she saw him, she would let out a small yelp of pain.

I started shivering. I didn't know if it was from having gotten cold and wet on the bike earlier or if it was the prospect of telling Cory's family their dog had died. They probably had a child. I thought of the kid crying and how his mother would dry his tears while the dad went down to the basement to look for a box to bury Cory in. All three of them would be sad together. They'd have a quiet dinner, interrupted by the child's outbursts of crying. They would talk about what a good life Cory had had and how they would love him forever. I imagined the dad digging a hole in the backyard. Once they put Cory in the box, they'd all bury him together.

If I wanted to be at the bus station on time, I'd have to bring Cory to his family right away. But I couldn't stop shivering. I looked up and down the road, hoping someone would come out of a house and help me. I suddenly felt weak and had to sit down on the curb.

A few minutes later, a car approached slowly. I didn't look up until the motor stopped right next to me, and the door opened. It was Ma.

"Wren!" she cried. "Are you all right? Did you have an accident?" She pulled me up. "You're bleeding! There's blood on your jacket."

"It's not my blood," I said. "It's from the dead dog. I found him by the side of the road." I pointed to Cory.

"He has a tag. I think his owners live right around the corner."

"Oh, baby," Ma said. "I'm so glad I found you."

"I was going to Chicago," I said. "I wanted to talk to that woman. I don't believe what you said about her. I don't want to think of Dad having done something like that. I just don't want to." Suddenly there wasn't enough space inside my chest, and I could only take small breaths. "And now . . . now I have to tell these people that their dog died. But I can't do it. I can't. It's too sad."

"You don't have to go to Chicago," Ma said, holding my shoulders. "And I'll go with you to meet Cory's owner."

I took enough air to ask the question I needed to ask. "Why didn't you tell me sooner that you were so mad at Dad because he had a girlfriend?"

"I'm so sorry," Ma said, and I could tell she was holding back tears. "It hurt me so much that he'd do that. That he'd leave me for another woman. I couldn't even believe they were sending each other real letters on fancy stationary. That's what we did when we first met. He was such a romantic." Her voice quivered, but she continued.

"It was like I was on fire with pain and anger and rage and more pain. I tried to get away from it all by taking us on the road. You were already so hurt. I didn't want to destroy your memories of him too."

"But . . ."

"I know it was wrong," she said. "In the end, I hurt you more, and we didn't talk at all. And, after a while, I didn't know how to tell you anymore."

"What about those other men?" I asked.

Ma shook her head. "I feel so stupid now. I wanted to know what it felt like. What it was like for him to be with somebody else. But it didn't work. I only hurt myself — and you — more. Oh, Wren, I've made so many mistakes. I hope you can forgive me."

I was startled for a moment. No one had ever asked me for forgiveness. I looked up at her. "Of course I'll forgive you. But it's still so hard to believe that Dad did this. I don't know how to . . . how to . . ."

"I know," Ma said. "It means we have to forgive him for what he did and mourn him. I don't know how to do that by myself either. But maybe we can do it together."

I fell into her arms, and Ma held me tight as I buried myself in her jacket. I could feel her lips on my hair. We stayed like that for a while, and I felt good and warm.

When I looked up at her, Ma gently pushed a strand of hair from my forehead. "Come on, baby. We'll bring Cory home."

41

Ma parked the car in front of a rundown house, and we walked up the stairs to the front door. The house was in bad shape. Shingles were missing from the siding, and the windows were so dirty I couldn't even tell if there were curtains inside or not. We had wrapped Cory in an old blanket that Ma had found in the trunk of her car. I held him in my arms while Ma knocked on the door.

"Hello," she called. But no one answered.

"I wonder if that's where they kept Cory," I said, pointing to a small cage on the far side of the porch. There was a filthy-looking rag inside, and when I stepped closer, I could see dog poop in the corner.

"It's gross," Ma said. "Look at the poop. They shouldn't lock him in there all day."

"He's not home yet," a woman's voice called. I turned. On the front porch of the neighboring house, a woman wearing a dark red housecoat and rollers in her hair stood smoking a cigarette.

"Do you know the family who lives in this house?" Ma asked.

"I sure do," the woman said. "But it's no family, just one guy. His name is Jeb Hamsun. He works at the casino. Won't be home until midnight."

"We found his dog," Ma said.

"Oh, that poor creature," the woman said, shaking her head. "Did that pooch finally run away?"

"I think so," Ma said. "My daughter found him on Easterday, run over by a car. He's dead."

Ma turned to me and rubbed my shoulder. I was still staring at that terrible cage.

"That poor dog might be better off dead," the woman said. "Jeb didn't seem to care much for him. I heard the little guy whimper in his cage day and night. I have no idea why Jeb even kept an animal." She took a drag from her cigarette. "I guess if the dog is dead, you've got to leave him out on the porch. I'll tell Jeb what happened."

"No, we can't leave him here!" I burst out, looking up at Ma.

"Don't worry. We won't leave him," Ma said. "We'll bury him."

"I'm not sure that's a good idea," the woman called. "Jeb might take that the wrong way."

"Well, that's too bad for Jeb," Ma said. "We wouldn't want to bother the man with the chore of giving his dog a proper burial if he didn't even care for him while he was alive."

* * *

"We should bury Cory at the pond," I said when we were back in the car.

"That's a good idea," Ma agreed, "but we need to get a shovel."

I didn't want to tell her that I had the trowel in my bag, so I let her stop and run into the tractor supply store while I waited in the car.

When we got to Pete's Pond, I gently lifted Cory out of the car. We found a clearing with a nice grassy spot under a pine tree. The ground was soft after the rain, and it didn't take Ma long until the hole was deep enough for me to put Cory inside it.

"It's sad what the woman said about Cory's life," I said.

"It sure is," Ma agreed. "But I'm glad we're doing this together."

We took turns shoveling the earth onto the blanket.

"Goodbye, Cory," I said when we were done.

"Goodbye, Cory," Ma echoed, putting her arm around my shoulder.

We stood there quietly for a while, and then I said, "I wish we could have buried Dad at least."

Ma nodded. "I didn't care about that for a long time." She pulled out a folded sheet of paper from her back pocket. "You asked me to send out the forms with our mailing address, and I never did. But I drafted a letter to the FAA. I was going to show it to you before you ran off."

The letter read:

Dear Sir or Madam,

I am the widow of Mr. Derek Kaiser, the passenger who died in the crash of Flight D8107 over the Atlantic near the North Carolina coast last February.

I have moved since the accident occurred, and I am sending you my forwarding address. I wanted to make sure you could contact me in the event that you were able to find my late husband's remains. My new address is . . .

"So you don't mind if they send us something of Dad's?" I asked.

"No," Ma said. "It wasn't right of me to just throw all his things out and drag you away. I'm sorry."

"I really hope they find something," I said. "Maybe his shoe or something from his briefcase. It'll be kind of corroded from the saltwater." For a moment I thought of the article I'd read about the decomposition of bodies immersed in the ocean. But I pushed those images away.

"That doesn't matter," Ma said. "It'll mean something to us."

42

That Friday, the township meeting room was crowded. I could tell that the township board hadn't expected so many local citizens to attend the meeting. There weren't nearly enough chairs in the town hall for all of them, and the room filled up quickly. In addition to Randle, Ma, and Mr. Leroy, I counted twenty people who had signed the petition and were now looking for a place to sit.

"Where's Mrs. Russo?" I asked Theo. "I thought she'd be here."

He shrugged. "I don't know, but I sure hope she comes."

Mr. Leroy leaned over to us. "The skinny man in the red tie who looks so nervous is the township supervisor, Mr. Kondrick," he said, pointing to the stage. "The others are the clerk, the treasurer, and the four trustees."

Mr. Zusack was one of the trustees, and he arrived with Carrie in tow. She looked lost standing there by herself near the windows. When the janitor had brought in enough chairs for the audience, the trustees took their seats, and the supervisor tapped on the table to open the meeting. We all got up to pledge allegiance to the flag, and then Mr. Kondrick approved the agenda.

At first it was very boring. They talked about a new stoplight and someone who needed permission to build a cell tower on 9 Mile Road. Then the supervisor called agenda item number six: "Rezone approximately eight acres near Pete's Pond to expand Pyramid's landfill."

The clerk read a short description of the project, and Mr. Kondrick asked the board members for their opinions.

Mr. Zusack said, "The landfill expansion is necessary and will benefit the community. The motion should be approved."

There was an unhappy murmur in the audience, and I was glad I had called the people who had signed the petition. The supervisor called the room to order, and the clerk announced that a petition had been submitted regarding the case. Then the supervisor asked if someone in the audience would like to speak.

Theo's dad stood up. "In the name of the citizens of Pyramid, we would like to express our opposition to the expansion," he said. "Instead of destroying a beautiful piece of nature to make space for more garbage, the community should explore ways to recycle and reduce waste."

People applauded, and Theo looked very proud.

"I think Robert Zusack has given us enough good reasons to support his measure," one of the trustees said. "Even in light of the dissenting voices, which is hardly a majority."

Someone in the audience shouted, "We need to be heard!"

The supervisor again called the room to order, and then our teacher, Mrs. Peters stood up. "I'd like to make the board aware of the fact that this voice of dissent originated from two middle school students who learned about the proposed expansion in class," she said. "They like to watch birds at Pete's Pond and have compiled an impressive series of photos that's still on display at the library. I believe that we're setting a bad example if we stifle their attempt to bring about change in their community."

Just then, Mrs. Russo came in. I caught her eye as she hurried toward the front, and she gave me a thumbs-up. She stopped behind my chair and handed me the turtle shell Theo and I had found, along with a sheet of paper. "Read this quickly and then tell the board."

The paper was a printout of an article about archaeological sites in the Upper Peninsula. Mrs. Russo had highlighted a portion of the text:

Turtle shells are found in ancient Native American burial grounds. They were used for rattles, with perforated holes tying the upper and lower shells together, and for attaching a handle. Ancient native people may have given these rattles to the dead in their graves . . .

In the margin Mrs. Russo had written, *If Pete's Pond is an ancient Native American burial ground, it cannot be destroyed!*

"We'll go ahead and vote on the matter," the supervisor said. "The motion will not be decided by referendum, but by a vote of the township board."

Mr. Zusack gave a satisfied nod, and I saw Theo's dad shake his head in disappointment.

"How can you just overrule the opinion of your citizens?" a young man called out from the back row.

"The board will vote on the motion," the supervisor reiterated.

I looked at Mrs. Russo, who nodded encouragingly. "I would like to say something, Mr. Kondrick," I said.

The room was suddenly quiet, and everyone stared at me. I had to force myself to keep breathing.

"We have found evidence that the area around Pete's Pond was used by ancient Native Americans as a burial ground," I announced.

Mr. Kondrick frowned at me. "What kind of evidence would that be?"

"Box turtle shells that were used by Native Americans as gifts to their dead. These shells were often made into rattles and then added to burial sites. We found one of those shells at Pete's Pond. We also have evidence of another shell that was discovered there earlier." I paused to take a breath. I was so nervous I could hear my heart beating.

"You mean the area around Pete's Pond could be an ancient Native American burial ground?" Mr. Zusack asked.

"Exactly," Randle added, standing up. "It also means that my people would like it to be preserved and not destroyed."

I looked at Theo and had to suppress a smile about the way Randle referred to the Chippewa as "his people."

"Your people?" Mr. Zusack asked.

"I am part Chippewa myself, and I know the tribe will support the archeological examination of the site," Randle said.

Mr. Zusack massaged his forehead with his right hand and suddenly looked very concerned. "But you don't know for sure," he said. "All you have is this one turtle shell."

"No, we also have evidence that another shell with the same kind of holes was found near the pond thanks to a photo taken by my father, Edward Redbird," Randle said.

Now the audience's murmur grew so loud that Mr. Kondrick had to call everyone to order again.

"You see these holes?" Randle had taken the shell from my hand and was holding it up. "They were most likely used to attach a handle to the rattle. The Chippewa still make these rattles and use them in ceremonies." He paused before continuing. "If finding these shells means that this is sacred ground to Native Americans, it cannot be debased by burying garbage in it."

"How come the tribe doesn't know about the site? The expansion plans have been publicized, and no one from the tribal council has claimed the land," Mr. Zusack said.

"We don't keep records of our burial grounds. Native Americans don't administer the dead," Randle said. "The shell is likely more than two hundred years old. At that time, Native Americans lived freely on the Upper Peninsula. Federal law protects Native American burial sites from further destruction. So, should the township give you permission to expand your business and proceed with your plan, the courts will decide. And" — Randle inhaled, making a dramatic pause — "I can assure you that this will be decided in favor of the Chippewa."

Mr. Zusack looked defeated. It was really hard not to gloat, and I had to make a fist so I wouldn't jump up and scream. Randle had explained this better than we ever could.

Mr. Kondrick whispered something to the trustee sitting next to him, who shook his head. "Well," Mr. Kondrick said, "we'll have to reconsider this motion in light of this new development. I suggest that the motion be dismissed until a further investigation into the matter has taken place. Those in favor of dismissal raise their hands."

The supervisor, the treasurer, the clerk, and the three trustees raised their hands. Mr. Zusack did not.

"Motion dismissed," said the clerk.

* * *

Outside, we thanked the people who had come to support us, but they mostly wanted to thank me. I told everyone that it was Mrs. Russo who had found the answer.

"But you spoke up," Theo's dad said. "And that's important."

When Randle joined us, I shook his hand. "Thank you very much," I said.

"Thank *you*," Randle replied.

"I am so proud of you," Ma said, walking up behind me and giving me a hug.

"Randle, this is my mom," I said. "Ma, this is Randle."

"I know," Ma said, smiling at Randle. "We've met at the retirement home. You certainly saved the day."

Randle smiled. "It was my pleasure."

Mrs. Russo joined us, and I gave her a hug. "Thank you so much," I said.

"I'm glad I could help," she replied. "But this wouldn't have happened without you and Theo." She turned to Randle and added, "And you spoke so well tonight. It sure helped that you're part Chippewa."

"He's also a Buddhist," I said. "But I'm sure the Buddha wouldn't mind you speaking up to save an ancient Native American burial ground."

Randle laughed. "I think he would understand. The Buddha is in favor of preserving the environment and wants us to live in harmony with nature. He definitely doesn't support unnecessary landfills."

43

"My dad doesn't think the landfill will be expanded," Theo said when we were back at Pete's Pond the following week. "An archeologist confirmed that the shell we found is really old and could be from a gravesite. He plans to file for permission to start a dig. And a group of his students is planning to petition the township to support more recycling. My dad said we started a movement."

"When we left the township meeting, I noticed that Mrs. Russo was talking to your dad for a long time," I said. "That look they gave each other at the farmer's market is apparently leading somewhere now?"

"I don't know," Theo said. "I hope it'll mean something."

"My mother told me that Randle asked her out for dinner," I said. "They met at the nursing home and then again at the township meeting. She wanted to know what I thought of them getting to know each other better."

"What did you say?"

I shrugged. "That's fine by me. I like Randle."

Loud cawing came from the forest behind us, and we both turned around to take a closer look.

"Look at all those crows gathering," Theo said, pointing his camera in their direction.

"There's a dead one lying on the ground," I told him, zooming in on it with my binoculars.

"All the others are sitting in the trees around it, screeching," Theo said.

"More are coming. It's almost like they're calling them to come to mourn," I said.

Soon the tree was filled with black birds. Then one of the perching crows swooped down and landed next to the dead crow. Others hopped closer, and soon a group of ten or twelve crows circled the dead bird.

"If a group of crows is called a murder," Theo said, watching through his camera, "is this a murder of crows mourning the murder of a crow?"

"I don't know," I said. "But it's kind of sad."

"I hope it's not your friend Joseph," Theo said.

"I don't think so," I said. "There's no white spot on its head."

"Oh, by the way, I brought you something," Theo said, pulling a digital camera from his backpack. "I know you said you didn't want it, but I think you're wasting your time with the drawings. I hate to break it to you, but you aren't getting any better."

I took the camera and looked through the finder. "I know. I was never much of an artist. Will you show me how to use it?"

"Of course," he said. "Let's start right now."

Theo showed me how to operate the zoom and which button to press to see the picture you'd just taken. I heard a blue jay and looked for its blue and white feathers in the trees. When I found it, I adjusted the camera until I could see the bird inside the frame. I zoomed in until the image was sharp, and clicked.

"Not bad for a beginner," Theo said, looking at the display. "We can go to my house later if you want. I'll show you how to download the photos. Then we can print out the best ones for your journal."

I nodded. The crows had ended their wake and flown off. Just one bird remained, lying still and quiet on the ground. I knew I wouldn't need to come back to bury it.

44

At the end of April, an envelope from the FAA arrived. Ma and I sat at the kitchen table, and I ripped it open. Inside was Dad's fountain pen. I opened the cap and unscrewed the top. There was also a letter, which I handed to Ma.

"The letter says that they found the pen a while ago and sent it to the pilot's widow," Ma said. "Since she returned it, they assumed it must be Dad's."

I placed the pen on the kitchen table, and we stared at it for a few minutes in silence. Finally Ma asked, "Remember when we bought it for him?"

I nodded. "The lady in the store looked like a Goth girl with her face powdered white and her eyebrows plucked to a thin black line."

Ma laughed. "You called her a fountain pen ghoul."

"Dad really liked that pen," I said. We were quiet again for a while, both of us just looking at our gift and thinking of Dad. It was good to remember him together, even without any words.

Eventually Ma picked up the pen and unscrewed the top. The silver tip was corroded. "What should we do with it?" she asked.

"There's still ink in it," I said, looking at her blue-stained fingertips.

"It probably still works," Ma said. She reached for a piece of paper and scribbled on it. "Just needs a little cleaning and fresh ink. Maybe we should each write a letter to Dad."

"I like that idea," I said. "We could put our letters in a box and take it to Lake Superior."

Ma smiled. "That's a good plan."

* * *

And that was exactly what we did. We each used the pen to write our letters. I wrote mine sitting on the boulder by the pond, listening to the birds.

Dear Dad,

They found your pen, and Ma and I are each writing you a letter.

I was sad to hear that you cheated on Ma. She was mad at you, so mad that she wouldn't even talk to me anymore. Your lie hurt both of us, even after you were gone. But I can't do anything about that, and the most important thing is that Ma and I are talking again. I hope in her letter, she can forgive you too.

We live in Pyramid, Michigan, now, and soon we'll have enough money to buy a house. I still watch birds and use the journal that you gave me, but I gave up trying to draw the birds that I see. I'm just not getting any better at it. Instead, I take photos of them for my journal. My friend Theo, who is a great photographer himself, gave me his old camera. We watch birds together quite a bit, and it's fun. I think you would like Theo.

I also have a job here in Pyramid. I work in a health food store with a Frenchman who is going to teach Ma how to cook. Yes, believe it or not, she's learning to cook — as in actually preparing a meal from scratch. Lots of things have changed but in a good way.

I still miss you and will always love you.
Wren

45

On a Sunday morning in early May, Ma and I drove out to Whitefish Bay on Lake Superior. It was a beautiful day, clear and calm, with only a few puffy clouds high up in the dark-blue sky. We parked near the lighthouse and walked to the beach.

Ma had called ahead, and the man we were renting the boat from was waiting at his dock when we got there. We stepped into the small green rowboat, and Ma took up the oars. I let my finger run through the freezing water.

When we were far enough out, Ma put down the oars, and we stayed still for a moment. I had brought along Dad's fountain pen, because the night before, I'd wondered if it was the same one he'd used to write love letters to that other woman. He had lived with this big fat lie — by cheating on Ma, he also had cheated on me.

"We should put the pen in the box," I said.

"Don't you want to keep it?" Ma asked.

I shook my head. "It's better to let it go."

Saying those words made me think of Randle. For a moment, I felt guilty about letting my mind wander to him while we were saying goodbye to Dad. But then I looked at Ma holding the box over the water. She smiled at me and opened it so I could add the pen next to the stones we'd put inside to make sure the box would sink.

"It would be better if we had his ashes," Ma said.

"I know," I said. "But this is all we have."

"We also have our memories," Ma said. "We'll hang on to those as well — the good ones at least."

"So can you think of him now without getting mad?" I asked.

She nodded. "Yes. As long as I think of all the good times that we shared."

I looked out on the water and quietly said, "I love you, Dad. Goodbye."

Ma whispered goodbye too and then slipped the box into the water. Together we watched it sink beneath the surface, out of sight.

After a moment, Ma bent forward to touch me, but the boat swayed dangerously and she had to catch herself. "I guess I'll hug you later," she said, and we had to laugh because it felt so clumsy.

We rowed back to shore, and when we were in the car again, Ma opened her purse, pulled out a folder, and put it on my lap. "I spoke to a realtor, and she gave me this list of possible houses for us. Want to go and look at them when we get back?"

"I sure do," I said.

Ma smiled and reached over to put her hand on mine. She started the car, and we drove east along Lakeshore Drive. Soon we passed a sign announcing: *Pyramid — 8 miles.*

Ahead, I saw an osprey take off from her nest in a tall pine tree and soar out over the bay, light and free. Watching the bird made me think of Theo. I was planning to meet him later at the boulder by Pete's Pond. He'd want to know about our morning at the lake, and I'd ask how his father's date with Mrs. Russo went. Then we would start birding.

I looked forward to getting home.

Monika Schröder

Monika Schröder grew up in Germany, but has worked in American international schools in Egypt, Oman, Chile, and India. Before moving to the United States in 2011, she was the elementary school librarian at the American Embassy School in New Delhi. Monika currently lives with her husband and dog in the Blue Ridge Mountains of North Carolina. *Be Light Like a Bird* is her fourth novel for young readers. You can visit her online at www.monikaschroeder.com.